BY THE
Book

MARIA VICKERS

By the Book

Maria Vickers

Copyright © 2017

ALL RIGHTS RESERVED

Cover Models:

Tank Joey

www.tankjoey.com

Connor Jay

Photographer: **CJC Photography**

www.cjc-photography.com

Cover Design: **T.E. Black Designs**

www.authorteblack.com

Editing: **Shana Vanterpool**

www.shanavanterpool.com/editing-services/

BY THE BOOK

by

Maria Vickers

Table of Contents

From the Author

I've always loved books. Not only creating stories, but reading them as well. Books transport me, and when I was younger, I would run into walls because I refused to put my books down even for a second. Take note, walking while reading is not advised. LOL.

With my books, I dream of sharing my stories with the world. I want others to be transported or to feel the emotions my characters feel. That is my goal. If I can do that for one person, I succeeded.

Getting sick changed me and my life, but it also opened doors that I thought were closed. Today, even though I may not be able to do as much as I once could, I still have my mind and I can write.

"…I hope that simple love and truth will be strong in the end. I hope that real love and truth are stronger in the end than any evil or misfortune in the world."

--Charles Dickens, David Copperfield

Chapter 1

Joshua

"What the hell is wrong with you?" my friend, Jacob, growled as he rolled off me and stood up. Grabbing the basketball shorts he had discarded before we climbed into bed, he jerked them on and then spun around to glare at me, his shorts tenting where his cock was still hard.

I sat up and questioned it all myself. What was wrong with me? I honestly didn't know. Jacob was the first friend I had made when I moved to attend Florida State University here in Tallahassee, FL, and while I was majoring in Biology with an emphasis in Marine Biology, he was majoring in Biology with an emphasis in plants. I always suspected he selected his major in order to learn how to grow marijuana, but I could never prove it, and I didn't bother to ask. Some classes overlapped, others did not, but he was always there for me whenever I needed. He supported me as a true friend and frat brother.

In a way, that was how he and I ended up in the sort of relationship we had. During my first semester, I was stressed out and worried that I wouldn't make it. The straw that broke the camel's back for me was when I received a failing grade on a major exam, and he was in the same boat. Freaked out over the test and anxious about school in general, we met up to complain to each other and wound up falling into bed and having sex for the first time. After that, whenever either of us were between men and needed a release, we called each other.

Today, I wanted to celebrate taking my last final for the semester and to blow off some pent-up frustration, and the moment his hand touched my dick, I shied away from him. That had never happened before. Jacob was hot and desirable. With his beach blond straight hair that reached his shoulders and his icy blue eyes that seemed to notice everything, I never had a problem with him touching me. I liked it when he touched me. His hands were calloused from waxing his surf board and working in his uncle's auto repair shop. The roughness always felt magical as his fingers squeezed and pulled.

So completely opposite of the man I dreamed of having. Maybe that was my problem. All day long, whenever my mind was not occupied with tests—and sometimes during those educational torture devices—Samuel Cayden entered my thoughts unbidden. For three years I tried to forget my high school biology teacher, tried to forget his dark curly hair and his hazel eyes. Tried to forget his tatted arms that were connected to a body that reminded me less of a surfer and more of a body builder.

I could close my eyes and imagine the feel of Sam's strong hands as they patted my back or squeezed my shoulder when I did something well. And I could see his knuckles turning white while holding a bat during practice, like when he coached my varsity baseball team to the state championship during my senior year. He was my coach, my teacher, my mentor, and the man I fell in love with. The one my heart refused to forget.

If I chose to be truthful, it was those thoughts of Sam that drove me to Jacob's place today, and those same thoughts that pushed Jacob away. I'd lost my mind. That was the only explanation. "Sorry," I muttered softly, both embarrassed and frustrated. I released a heavy sigh and let my head fall back against the wall with a soft thump.

"Want to talk about it?" he asked. Before he was my friend with benefits, he was first and foremost my friend. One I'd like to keep if at all possible.

I didn't know if I could talk to him about this, though. For three years, I pretended as if Sam never existed in my quest to bury his memory. Too bad my head and heart never got the memo. "Nah."

"Josh, come on, man. Tell me what's wrong, because this is fucked up."

I pondered which part he meant: me fucking him to forget my teacher, or me pushing him away because I couldn't stop thinking about that same man. I sat there on the bed, looking at the ceiling, unable to meet Jacob's gaze, and finally asked, "Have you ever been in love?"

"Nope, and I doubt it will happen any time soon. I'm having too much fun being single." He laughed.

I couldn't join in.

"Josh? What's wrong?"

A weight I'd carried since I left my tiny town of Imperial, Missouri suddenly got heavier, crushing me. "I have." I finally focused on him, and said, "I still do."

"Dude! Why didn't you say something? What the fuck are you even doing here? You should get him to fuck you into next week." His chastisement hit me in the gut.

"He's back home."

"Back home? You mean you two broke up because you couldn't do long distance or something?"

"Not exactly." Laughter bubbled up and spilled out. Not even a hint of amusement could be heard in it, because it held nothing except contempt and pain. Tears burned my eyes and I squeezed them shut, but as soon blackness engulfed my vision, I saw Sam standing there smiling at me, his beard bushy and soft. I remembered touching it a couple of times when I thought I could get away with it. He always gave me a funny look whenever I did it, but never discouraged or stopped me. Maybe it would have been better if he had.

"Then what?" Jacob prodded.

Sighing, I slowly opened my eyes, taking in the sight of his blond hair gleaming in the sunlight streaming through the window. He'd laugh at me if I told him that in that moment, he almost looked like a glowing angel; like in that TV show my mom used to make me watch with her when I was a kid, Touched by an Angel.

I bumped my head against the wall behind me again. "We weren't together. Not allowed. Not wanted. Not—"

"What the hell are you rambling about? You're a great guy and anyone would be lucky to have you. Did your parents forbid you like some Romeo and Juliet bullshit?"

I barked with laughter. "No, nothing like that." I took a deep breath and then opened myself up to confess. "He was my high school teacher."

"We've all had our crushes."

"I wish this was nothing more than a crush. Maybe it started out that way, but not anymore. It's more than that. So much more, and the pathetic thing is, I still love him."

He sat on the bed next to me, him in his shorts, me still naked as the day I was born. Throwing one arm around my shoulders, he pulled me close. "It's not pathetic, but what is pathetic is trying to find a substitute when only the real one works."

"Pun intended?" I snickered.

"Oh yeah," he drawled. We both laughed.

For the first time since I left home, I felt lighter, freer. Maybe I only needed to talk about it all to let go. I wasn't over Sam by a long shot, but maybe now with time it was possible. I apparently loved to delude myself with little lies like that.

"How about we go out, grab some pizza and beers to celebrate a temporary reprieve from our academic torture, and then we'll go find some trouble. My treat," Jacob offered.

The man had a sixth sense about things sometimes, and that sounded like the perfect way to get my mind off of a certain someone. "I'm in."

"But first, you have to get up and get dressed. While I don't mind looking at your naked ass all night, Tallahassee isn't a nudist commune," he joked.

Rolling my eyes, I shook my head at him as I grabbed the pillow that lay beside me. Holding it firmly, I swung and hit him in the face before scrambling off the bed, laughing again. "You're just afraid people will appreciate my naked ass more than yours."

"Ha! In your dreams." He got off of the bed and nudged me on his way to change into better clothes than the athletic shorts he wore.

Tonight would be good. I'd forget about Sam, temporarily, and have some fun. And maybe one day, I wouldn't have to pretend or lie to myself any longer.

***

Two pitchers of beer, two shots, and five hours later, I could no longer lie to myself about anything. I had been summoned home.

"Josh, I'm sorry to be calling you when you're at school, but an ambulance came and took your mother to the hospital," my mom's neighbor, Mrs. Byrd, informed me. I'd almost ignored the call, but something nagged at me when I saw the 636 area code, and I answered it before it got dumped into voicemail.

I stood in the middle of a college bar, playing a game of pool, and nursing a good buzz, but her words had the power to sober me up. My mother was as healthy as a horse and was never sick a day in her life. "Are

16

you sure?" That was a stupid question. The two houses were only twenty feet from each other. If an ambulance had shown up Mrs. Byrd would know.

"I'm very sure. You need to come home," she instructed me.

Stunned silence answered her. I didn't know what to say, or how to speak.

I heard her harrumph. "Joshua Dayton? Did you hear me?"

"Y-Yeah, I heard you. I'll come." I hung up the phone and looked at Jacob. "I have to go home."

He didn't say anything. He dropped his cue on the table and led me out of the bar. I was still too drunk to drive, but I could go back to my apartment and start packing.

I hadn't been back home since I ran away to college almost three years ago. I never planned on returning, but now I had been called back and couldn't ignore the request.

Chapter 2

Joshua

Exhaustion wrapped its tentacles around my body and held it prisoner by the time I pulled up to my mother's house. I hated flying. I could do it and had flown a few times before, but that didn't mean I liked it. The mere thought of being in a hollow metal tube suspended high in the air didn't sit right with me, no matter what the statistics said. If I was going to be in an accident, I'd much rather it be on the ground where I had a chance of walking away from it. Statistics could kiss my ass.

Nothing had changed since I left. The red brick house my parents claimed for their own stood beside others that resembled everything about it. The only thing different from house to house was the plants and furniture people selected. My mother's had a porch with red brick columns, and the house was longer than it was wide. Old houses in Missouri all seemed to be made that way. Two small concrete steps led to a small space where a swing sat on one end and ferns on the other.

From the porch, it took exactly one step to walk into the living room. Off to one side would be a short hallway that led to two different bedrooms, and to the back straight through the living room, would be the kitchen, the back door, and the staircase that led to the basement. All of the houses around here had basements. For me, that's where my bedroom had moved to when I got older. Somehow my mother knew a teenager didn't want to sleep right across from his parents at night. Three feet, bedroom door to bedroom door. No one in their right mind would want to sleep that close to their parents.

The summer before my freshman year in high school, they remodeled the house making the kitchen more open and finishing the basement to give me my own space. If I would have thought about it, or maybe if I hadn't found Sam, I could have used that space to my advantage. The back door stood at the top of the stairs. It would have taken no effort whatsoever to sneak out the back or sneak someone into my domain. I never did either of those though.

I hadn't left Tallahassee until almost midnight, giving myself a few hours to sober up, and drove all night to get to my mother. When I was only about an hour away, I called the hospital and found out they had released her. It made me wonder if Mrs. Byrd overreacted. It could've been anything, or nothing at all. So instead of driving to Festus and the hospital, I drove past that town and continued the drive down the highway until I reached Imperial.

It truly was Small Town USA with its main street overrun with old shops and buildings that stood long before I was born, small population—something they loved to brag about—and people who sometimes dressed like they were in the wrong decade. That was not to say the city didn't boast anything modern; it did. It couldn't remain outdated forever when St. Louis was only about fifteen minutes away. When you exited, one side of Interstate 55 was like stepping into another era, while the other side boasted all modern buildings. They were fewer and had more space on the modern side, and also managed to have a lot less traffic.

And now I sat in my car in front of my house. I was almost certain Mrs. Byrd watched me from her perch in her window. She would come over later and pretend she wasn't the nosey neighbor she most definitely was. I swore she could give the neighbors in any old sitcom a run for their money.

I should go in, but I was scared. In high school, I lost my father when he had a heart attack. And even though I told myself it couldn't be anything serious if the hospital discharged her, I was still scared that something would happen to my mother as well. If I sat there, I could pretend that nothing was wrong for a little longer.

Taking in a deep cleansing breath, I glanced over to Mrs. Byrd's house and almost laughed when I saw the curtain move slightly. I spotted a spy. Something about that settled me.

With some lingering trepidation, I got out of my car and took a sweeping glance of my old neighborhood before I slowly placed one foot in front of the other and forced myself to go home. That short trip from the car to the door, shuffling up the cracked walkway that led to the house, gave me more anxiety than anything I'd dealt with at FSU.

One more deep breath when I reached the porch, and I opened the door to step inside, and stopped with only one foot in, frozen in my tracks. Across the living room, in the kitchen, leaning against the island, stood the one man I had been trying to get away from.

We stared at each other, both too shocked to move. I pulled my other foot inside and dropped the bag in my hand. It landed with a loud thud. Yes, Imperial was probably one of the smallest towns around. Yes, Sam lived in the same small town and taught at the local high school, but that did not mean I expected to see him in my house, standing in my mother's kitchen. If I managed to run into him, I would've sworn it'd be around town or at a restaurant, not here.

Neither of us broke eye contact. I hadn't seen him in three years, but right now, it felt as if that time had not separated us. All I could think about was the letter I wrote him, the one I shoved in his hands after graduation had come to a close. I left for Florida the next day. Had he read it? I wanted to know, and yet, at the same time, I wanted to pretend I was never that bold.

Much like the house, he hadn't changed. His white t-shirt pulled tight across his chest, and I could see his tattoos disappearing underneath his sleeves. The tattoos covered one arm completely, while the other one only had a half-sleeve. I also knew that he had ink that covered his back and one leg. There was something sexy about a man covered in color. Actually, it was only this man. Others with tattoos did nothing for me. It was only Sam.

In my dreams, I could picture it all so clearly. The colorful swirls of pictures flowed over his skin from his upper back to his ankles, his skin alive with vivid color. I'd dreamed of kissing every inch of paint.

Samuel Cayden appeared as if by magic in my life as a sophomore. This was the man I had been thinking about yesterday, the reason I pushed Jacob away. And now he stood less than fifty feet from me.

"I'm…I'm glad you came," he said, his voice gruff and tight.

I pondered his words for a moment. Had he expected me to abandon my only family, my mother? "My mother needs me, where else would I be?" I swallowed hard and then dismissed him, "Thank you for helping out, you can go now." I had to get away from him so I could breathe again. Being around him, seeing him again after I left without a backward glance, messed with my equilibrium. My emotions intensified and crashed down upon me with a vengeance. Leave, please leave, I silently prayed. I didn't know why he was here. I couldn't occupy the same space as him right now.

"I uh…" he started to say. His lips turned downward and his eyes appeared haunted and sad.

"Samuel," a soft, muffled, feminine voice called out from somewhere to my left. I knew that voice: my mother. It sounded weaker than I remembered. And it had called for my old teacher.

"I'll be right there," he answered loudly, never taking his eyes off me.

Samuel? I'd like to know when my mother started calling my old teacher by his first name. Up until the point I'd left, it'd always been Mr. Cayden, but then again, I hadn't been aware that they'd kept in touch.

A soft knock startled us and we finally broke eye contact. Sam cleared his throat. "Why don't I get that? Your mom will want to see you," he suggested. His voice still sounded tight and unsure. His forehead was wrinkled slightly from his small frown, and his eyes darted from me to the direction of my mother's bedroom door.

"You know what my mom wants?" I asked snidely.

"I—" Another knock at the door interrupted him. "Go and check on your mom," he directed as he came toward the door, his hand raking through his thick hair.

Moving away from the door to give him space, our chests accidentally brushed, and the spark of electricity I tried to forget, ignited, stopping me in my tracks. Three years apart and I still craved him like no other. My breath caught and my skin felt alive as my heart thumped harder and louder. I wanted to reach out and grab him and at the same time, shove him out the door so that I didn't have to see him, didn't have to be around him.

His Adam's apple bobbed and my eyes zeroed in on that part of his body. I wondered what it would be like to lick it, to suck on it until we were both writhing with desire.

Shaking my head to clear it, I moved toward my mother's bedroom, trying to forget him and the plethora of emotions coursing through my body. But I stopped when I heard Mrs. Byrd's voice. "Did he make it back yet? Have you heard from Josh?" Her question sounded anxious. Not sure why since she knew exactly when I pulled up to the house.

"Yeah, he just got here," he answered her. His words were terse and suddenly sounded exhausted. For the first time, I wondered if he had been with my mother when the ambulance was called and was taken to the hospital. I didn't want to think what it meant if that were true, because I could already feel the burn in my stomach growing.

"Good. I don't know why you didn't call him. He needs to be home with his mother," she chastised Sam. I almost laughed. Hearing a man who was thirty-five get scolded like a child, was hilarious. "That's the only parent he has left. I know you said I didn't have to call him, but he should be here." Now she was starting to sound like a broken record. Why was it that when someone was chastising another, the repeat button was hit?

"She's fine. He didn't need to be called."

"Where is she?"

"Resting. We didn't get home from the hospital until early this morning."

"Good. That's where she should be."

Listening to this conversation, I realized I still didn't know what was wrong with the woman I'd driven all night for. I mean, she and I didn't necessarily see eye to eye, but she was still my mother, and my only family since my father passed away.

"You know what I think?" Mrs. Byrd asked.

I stood just in the hallway, which was only long enough to accommodate a door on each side and the bathroom door straight ahead. When I heard that, I turned in enough time to peer around the corner and watched as Sam rubbed a hand over his face. "No, but I bet you're going to tell me," he grumbled.

"You should marry her. That will do more for her than coming by and helping her fix things around this old house."

My focus zeroed in on those words, marry her. The mere thought of Sam as my step-father made my head spin and my stomach rebel, threatening to empty anything that might be in it—it wasn't much. No, marriage was not an option. Not my mother. Not Sam. I knew I didn't have a chance with him, but marriage between them had to be some sort of sick joke.

Those words echoed in my ears. I felt dizzy and out of breath. I should ignore the conversation, block out everything she said, and sit with my mother, but I couldn't do it. I couldn't go in that room and sit with my mother in my current state of disbelief and anguish.

Ignoring him, the neighbor, and everything else, I pushed past them and ran away again.

I ran without direction, and when I finally took the time to notice where I was, I found myself in the park a couple of blocks away from the house. This place with its luscious green trees and picnic tables used to be my happy place. My father brought me here when I was younger and we would practice playing catch or flying a kite. Those were happier times.

Four years ago, during the end of my junior year in high school, my father died of a heart attack. Neither my mother nor I expected it, but then again, who did expect something like that. Thankfully, we had the life insurance and my mom made a good living working as a financial advisor for a big company. We were able to mourn without worrying about our house, the bills, or anything else many people stressed over. In that sense—only that sense—we were lucky.

My father had always been my best friend, and the one person I could confide in no matter the situation. When I told him I was gay, he wrapped his arms around me and told me, "It'll be all right." I wasn't stupid and neither was he. We lived in a small, predominantly catholic community that didn't always like people or things that were "different," but with his support, I felt safe.

He was the one that broke the news to my mother, and she in turn cried and screamed. For years before that night, my mother and I'd had a strained relationship, and after that, although we remained cordial to each other, things between us were shaky at best.

Richard Dayton played such a huge role in my world, and when he disappeared, it was like a part of me went missing too. In one fell swoop, I lost my father, my best friend, and my cheerleader. I no longer had someone who came to all of my home baseball games in order to cheer me on, and I no longer had that one person in my corner whom I could count on and trust implicitly. I was alone.

My mother mourned the loss of her husband, and never tried to step up to the plate to replace him. She never came to my games and only came to events that had to do with me when it was considered necessary. Part of it was probably the fact she didn't know how to cope with losing the love of her life, and the other, I wasn't sure if she ever knew how to deal with me. Of course she always said it was because she had more important things to be concerned about, like making a living for both of us. My dad had life insurance when he passed away and my parents had savings, but we were now down to one income. She was the one that always worried about money, while my father had been more of the mindset that money wasn't everything.

After he died, I wanted to be alone. I stopped getting involved, hanging out with my friends, and skipped school. My friends tried to reach out, and I would act as if I was all right, but I was so lonely. It was that double edged sword. I both embraced solitude and hated it.

Until Mr. Cayden. Sometimes it was a simple pat on the shoulder or a word of encouragement at the right time that could break through a wall. He always seemed to know when I struggled the most, and was always there when I needed him.

It would be easy to say that my feelings for him were nothing more than the desire to have a father figure in my life, but whoever thought that would be wrong. From the moment I laid eyes on Sam, he captured my heart completely.

Chapter 3

Samuel

Seeing Josh again was a nightmare and a sweet dream all rolled into one.

I figured when I did eventually see him again that it would be under completely different circumstances. And now thanks to the old bat, Mrs. Byrd, he showed up out of the blue as if materializing from my subconscious.

When I heard the door open, I dropped my drill and spun around in surprise. No one was expected, and a typical person didn't just waltz in without permission. My breath caught and my heart seized as I stumbled backward a step, my back hitting the island behind me. It'd been almost three years since I'd seen him last. Fifty-four more days and it would have been, but who was counting.

He'd changed since he left. I could still see the teen he'd been. He was still tall and lanky, but he had filled out, his muscles giving him more form. His dark brown hair had grown out, and now it fell in rich waves over his eyes. It suited him. But he hadn't changed completely. His eyes, they were still the same brown soulful eyes I remembered captivating me when he was a student.

God help me. I told myself countless times how wrong it was to fall in love with a student, but I still fell down that rabbit hole.

"What has gotten into that boy? I can remember when he loved it when you came over. You were his favorite teacher in school, you know. Must be that college. They party down there in Florida all the time. It must have messed with his brain," Mrs. Byrd chided haughtily. Her once black hair had more salt than pepper. Her face was haggard and old, with an oversized nose and crooked teeth. For some reason, she always reminded me of a witch from movies, only she wasn't green.

"I'm sure he's just overwhelmed." I tried to push her out the door, but I think I would've had more success moving a mountain. "After you told him about the ambulance, he must have driven all night."

"That's what planes are for."

"He doesn't fly."

"What…I mean, that's all well and good. At least he's here now."

I lifted one of my eyebrows in disbelief. This woman annoyed me on a good day, and today, I wanted to throw her into a bottomless pit and walk away. "Alice wanted him to focus on school, that's why she didn't call him."

"Well, he needs to be with his mother," she repeated, her voice reminiscent of nails on a chalkboard. "If you ask me, he should have gone to college a lot closer to home. He's the man of the house now, and he should be here taking care of her instead of you."

I bit my tongue because if not, I would have lashed out. Mentally, I counted to five and then tried to speak calmly. My students didn't push my buttons like this woman. "For his major, it's better if he's at a coastal school."

"Isn't he majoring in biology? That's what Alice told me."

"Marine biology. He wants to study animals that live in water."

"We have lakes."

Don't take the bait. She is only trying to get you to argue, I warned myself. "In Tallahassee, he has access to a variety of marine life that he can study. He's in one of the best programs in the country."

"But…Whatever. At least he's home now."

I shook my head, refusing to justify her statement with an answer. We'd be here all day arguing our points if I didn't shut up. "Thank you for checking on Alice and Josh. Now, if you will excuse me, I really should check on the patient." I smiled politely, silently begging her to leave.

She eyed me warily, but finally huffed. "Be sure to call me if you need anything. Tell Alice I stopped by, and for her to call me later."

"I'll be sure to do that." She took two steps away from the door, and I shut it before she could change her mind. That woman could make a priest take the Lord's name in vain.

Leaning heavily against the door, my thoughts turned to Josh. When he heard her suggestion, I heard him gasp. I'd glanced at him and saw his large, wide eyes and clenched jaw before he dropped his head. His lips had been pinched and his nostrils were flaring with each noisy breath he took. He was either angry or pained by the casual recommendation.

26

Thanks to the big mouth neighbor, he probably assumed a lot of wrong things, and I wasn't sure how to fix them. I could tell him the truth, and yet, I wasn't sure he'd believe me.

Besides, he had a new life in Florida. I was nothing more than his old high school science teacher. I laughed at my own folly. I'd assumed things myself, like even though we were apart, nothing would change. Everything changed, and it was best that it had. He should be with someone his own age. Not someone fourteen years older than him.

***

Joshua

I didn't know how long I sat in the park, but when I finally became aware of my surroundings again, the sky had darkened, the crickets chirped, and a chill ran through me from the dropped temperatures. It might have been warmer earlier in the day from the mid-April sun, but as soon as the sun disappeared, so did the warmth.

Or maybe the coldness resided deep within me.

I'd lost him twice now.

I laughed at myself. Lost him? I never had him. As a sophomore, I fell in love at first sight. Although many would argue it was nothing more than a schoolboy crush. In my junior year, I had him for Biology II, and while he was hard and I had to make up a few of my tests for failing grades, he was fair and he taught me a lot.

My feelings grew.

After I lost my father during the end of my junior year, I couldn't focus and started sliding backward. Grades slipping, skipping classes, mouthing off to teachers—I was on a downward spiral. Samuel grabbed my hand, pulled me to safety, and remained close to me after that, making sure I behaved and didn't backslide. Never crossing the line—not that he wanted to or ever would.

He didn't even know how I felt about him until that damned letter. Why I thought I could write down my confession and then never see him again, is beyond me. It should've worked like I planned, but my luck tended to veer toward the bad side.

~~Dear Mr. Cayden,~~ Sam,

    I've gone back and forth about delivering this letter to you a million times. I've written and re-written it just as much. Once you read this letter, you will probably say something about it being natural for me to be confused, or that it is only a crush. It isn't that. I've known that I loved you for a while now, and even told my dad before he died. His advice was to think about it some more and to keep it to myself until at least after graduation. Which is why you are getting this now. I love you. It's not something I planned or expected, but there it is. I fell for you during my sophomore year, and now that I'm about to walk across that stage as a graduate, my feelings are stronger than ever.

    However, by the time you read this letter, I'll be gone. I'm leaving immediately for Florida. I won't be back. I honestly don't think I can face you now that I told you. Call me a coward if you want, but I don't want to hear you say that I'm confused or I don't know what love really is, or any number of other things. After I leave, I'll bury my feelings and pretend that they no longer exist. Maybe one day, I won't have to pretend any longer.

    Go and have an amazing life, find someone and fall in love. You deserve it. Thank you for everything.

~~Sincerely,~~ Love,
Joshua Dayton

For whatever reason, after I forced him to take my written confession, I convinced myself—naively—I would never have to face him again. There was always the possibility if I came home, but I had zero intentions of ever returning to Imperial, MO.

Except now, here I was, and I found him standing in my mother's kitchen, and chances were good that he was probably waiting on me to return after I stormed out earlier. Unfortunately for me, I couldn't stay in the park all night in order to avoid him.

Besides, the main reason I'd come home in the first place was for my mother. I drove all night to check on her, and in the end, I abandoned her without a second thought until now.

Slowly, I got to my feet, groaning as my muscles protested. I'd been sitting on the hard green wooden bench for too long.

Strolling back to my mother's house, I took my time. Even though I wanted to see her, I wasn't in any hurry to see him. It hurt too much. Instead, I gazed up at the stars and thought of my dad. He taught me all he could about astronomy, buying me my first telescope when I was five. The diamonds suspended in the sky were eventually replaced by a baseball diamond, but every summer, my dad and I would spend some time near the Meramec River and stargaze. God, how I wished he was here right now to talk me through this mess.

Selfish. That was me with a capital S. My mother was lying in bed sick, and I was more concerned about my own heart than her. I drove all the way from Florida, thinking about what Mrs. Byrd had said, and one look at that man drove all other thoughts out of my head.

It didn't take me long to arrive back at the house, and I noticed as I paused next to the cement walkway that led to the house, the front door was open wide. The old, creaky screen door blocked the bugs that would otherwise get in and the front porch light was shining brightly. Actually, all of the lights were on, and framed by the large picture window stood Sam…Mr. Cayden.

He never gave me permission to call him by his first name, but I recalled him telling a few people his name when he introduced himself. In my head, I immediately started calling him by his first name and nothing else.

His body was shadowed by the lights shining behind him, but the porch light gave his face a little illumination, and told me he was watching the street intently. His arms were folded over his chest and his eyes were drawn together in a frown. He waited for me to return after I ran away, throwing a jealous tantrum.

Swallowing hard, I turned to shuffle down the path, never taking my eyes off of him. I couldn't. His muscles pulled his shirt tight, and his hair was wet as if he'd taken a shower. But it was more than his body or seeing him standing there. Since high school, something about him had always drawn me to him, like a bug to a light, and I still felt that pull.

My hand shook as I grabbed the door handle, and suddenly my mouth felt as dry as the desert. How was I supposed to go in there and pretend Mrs. Byrd's words hadn't affected me, that seeing him didn't mess with my head? Books always made it sound like moving on from heartache was easy—I might have a secret passion for a good cheesy romance—that they could endure whatever and face anything. But that

29

was all bullshit. This was not easy. This was hard. It tore at me, ripping me to shreds. Three years passed, and I never stopped loving him. I wasn't sure I ever would.

"Everything all right?" He looked almost pained asking me that simple question after I found the courage to actually open the door and enter.

No, it wasn't. My anger, frustration, and hurt boiled close to the surface, and I had to hold back on what I wanted to say and do to him, while my body thrummed with anticipation being around him.

He took a step forward. "Josh—"

"How's my mother?" I cut him off. I didn't want to hear what he had to say.

His shoulders slumped as he glanced at the hall where the two bedrooms were situated. "She's fine. The doctors said it's the flu and she was dehydrated."

"The flu?" I asked incredulously. I'd heard of cases sending people to the hospital, but I never expected to hear that my own mother was taken down by something so normal. "Why wasn't I called?"

"She didn't want to worry you or bother you while you were dealing with school."

It may have been unfair, but I wondered if it was she didn't want to bother me, or she didn't want to bother with me. Since I'd left, we'd only talked a dozen or so times. There were no tears shed or any pleas for me to postpone my departure when I decided to leave right after I graduated. Not from her. "And you just happened to be here?"

"I was helping her fix a few things around the house."

"Well, aren't you handy?" I instantly regretted my tone and my words, but I wouldn't take them back. Although, I didn't know how I held my ground after I saw his chin lift a little and his hands curl into fists. Maybe I was too prideful for my own good.

"Your mother is resting in bed. I'm going to grab my tools and head home," he stated abruptly. As he headed to the kitchen, I caught the slight roll of his eyes, and I felt like a horse's ass when he grabbed a rusted metal toolbox from where it sat.

"Sam...I mean, Mr. Cayden, I'm sorry. I'm just really tired right now." I tried to offer some sort of apology, a peace offering.

My stubbornness and jealousy had gotten in my way.

***

Samuel

Hearing him call me by my nickname made my body heat up with desire. It sounded so natural, so perfect coming from his lips in a way it never did with anyone else.

I could see how tired he was with his bloodshot eyes and hair that looked like he'd run his hands though it a few hundred times. And after Mrs. Byrd's impromptu visit, it made sense that he would be on edge. That said, I didn't appreciate his condemnation. Everything I did, I did for him, and I would not allow him to talk to me as if I was no one or nothing. "Get some sleep." I stopped myself there, because the last thing I wanted to do was to get in a fight with him.

"Yeah," he said and spun on his heel, disappearing through the kitchen. I could hear a door open and close before I heard the patter of feet on the steps. Once he was gone, I dropped my head and tried to regain some sort of equilibrium. Josh had left and come back, and even though I knew he wasn't the same person I used to coach in baseball, something about him still sang melody to my harmony.

In three years, it should have been easy to forget him. I'd had tons of students, some more memorable than others, but no one touched something deep within me like Josh had. He was different. Special. And as much as I noticed him back then, the man I saw today had the power to draw all eyes to him.

He had grown up and matured, even if he was acting like a spoiled brat today.

As I gathered my tools, I thought about the last day I saw him. Graduation. I'd been required to be there, but for him, I think I would've shown up anyway. Josh Dayton was different than any of my other students for a few reasons. Most—not all—students wanted to coast through school, graduate, and move on to college to get away from their parents. Some were brilliant and could quote you the text book. Josh couldn't quote the text book, but his thirst for knowledge surpassed other students. No one could match it—then or now.

31

He loved biology. Not only the dissecting part, because honestly half the students who ever took my class loved that part, especially the guys, but he wanted to know how everything worked. He wanted to understand it all, and he sopped it up like a sponge, especially anything that had to do with water life. So when he told me he'd chosen to major in Marine Biology, I hadn't been surprised.

And then there was his personal life. I always got the impression he wasn't close to his mother. Anytime there was some sort of function the parents should attend, Josh's father arrived alone. In addition, Josh would talk about his dad and not his mom at all.

Suddenly, his world crashed down around him. His father died during Josh's junior year. Any time I tried to call his mother, she would blow me off and say that her son was in mourning. I understood that. I'd lost my own mother during my freshman year in college, but Josh had so much potential and deserved to have someone in his corner helping him through this. I stepped up to the plate.

After that, I started to become more aware of him. The way his short brown hair held a hint of wave, or how his smile had the power to infuse everyone around him with happiness. He was goofy, and yet rebellious. Smart and a slacker at times. And when he finally started to move forward again, he was the person everyone turned to for friendship, a good laugh, or just because he was a magnet that pulled people toward him.

The letter that he hurriedly thrust at me after graduation changed everything, and nothing at the same time. I'd pocketed the envelope without reading it at first, greeting other students, families, and faculty.

It wasn't until I was going through the suit to take to the dry cleaners a couple of days later, that I found that crumpled white envelope in my pocket again. My pants fell to the floor, forgotten. I fell on my bed holding it in my hand. I was unsure what it contained, and yet, I was almost afraid to open it. How had I forgotten something so significant for two days? Significant simply because it came from Josh. After graduation, I came home, changed, and then drove to the YMCA in Arnold for the graduation party hosted by the school. A lock-in that would allow the kids to party without alcohol. They had the facilities to themselves.

Josh didn't come. I watched and waited, but he never showed up, and I remembered feeling disappointed. Every time a car pulled up or a student arrived, I held my breath in anticipation. I didn't know why I did that. It wasn't like we could be together back then. Even before I read the letter, I knew he'd be leaving for college at some point over the summer to get settled in, and at the time I wasn't certain how he felt about me. Sure, there were moments I thought, this kid has a crush on me, but they flitted away almost as soon as I thought them, because if I held onto them too tightly, I was terrified of what would happen.

By the time I made it home from the party the next morning, I was exhausted and only wanted to sleep. The envelope sat forgotten in my pants pocket five feet away from me as I closed my eyes.

When I found it again, I sat there staring at the envelope in my hands for several minutes, the seconds ticking by in the background thanks to my antique alarm clock. One with two bells that had the ability to wake up the neighborhood with its loudness.

My name was scrawled on the front in Josh's messy handwriting. More than once, his teachers had to ask him what he'd written for an answer because it was so messy, he could give a doctor a run for his money. In fact, it was due to him that many teachers instituted a rule on any handwritten work and tests they gave: all answers had to be legible. Not exactly Josh's strong suit, but his handwriting had improved...slightly.

I finally turned it over and used my finger to push through the seal. My heart raced and my mouth suddenly felt very dry. I ripped the envelope when I hurriedly pulled out the letter and let the envelope float to the ground as my eyes slowly read the words Josh wrote me.

I wanted to hold onto each word written on the paper, and then, I wanted to ignore or pretend that Josh hadn't just told me that he was gone. Gone. It was funny. Reading that he loved me, it felt almost freeing, but knowing he left, hefted weight on me I wasn't sure I could bear.

The letter became balled and fisted inside my hand after I read his words. He loved me and he disappeared. It was written in his messy handwriting in blue ink that gave me a small thrill and punched me in the gut at the same time.

I'd already started to realize my feelings for him, but reading that letter, things suddenly became clear. The one thing I hadn't counted on nor wanted to happen, had come true. I'd fallen for a student. Ex-student.

Almost three years later, I still harbored the same feelings for him.

Grabbing the cold silver handle of my metal toolbox, my eyes drifted toward Josh's door and stayed there trying to see through the wood and plaster, but I wasn't Superman and I didn't have X-ray vision. Instead, I walked over to his door, intent on knocking. I raised my fist, brought it down, and stopped just short of the door. Instead of pounding on the door, I flattened my hand against the white wood and let it rest there for a minute. It was better this way. Better that he ran away. His life was in Florida, and mine...mine was here in this little town almost 800 miles away from him.

Chapter 4

Joshua

I'd done it again. In high school, I hid my feelings. After I graduated, I ran away to Florida and tried to forget him. And tonight, I ran away to the park and then down to my old room, hiding like an idiot until he left.

My heart pounded as I noticed the shadows of his feet under the door. I stood at the bottom of the stairs watching him, holding my breath, wanting him to simultaneously open the door and leave me alone. I wasn't ready or prepared to see him.

When the shadows disappeared, I waited until I heard his feet march across the upstairs and out the door before I climbed the stairs again. "Coward," I mumbled to myself as I stuck my head around the corner to make sure Samuel had indeed left the house. He was just a man and I should be able to face him, but I couldn't. I kept hiding, and in doing so, I disregarded his importance.

Slowly, I made my way through the house, looking at the pictures hanging on the walls and the little knickknacks scattered throughout the living room. A few things were new, but for the most part, everything had remained the same. This was the house I grew up in, the house where I had so many happy memories from my childhood until high school. Everything changed after we lost my father. My mother and I were more strangers than family, but we managed to coexist.

Being in this house again, my chest felt tight and my body acted like it was on high alert as my gaze swept side to side. Samuel wasn't the only reason I ran away, but at the same time, she was still my mother and I did love her.

This house brought back so many memories, however, at the end of my junior year, it became nothing more than brick and mortar. There was a patch in the plaster near the front door. It'd been painted over to match the rest of the living room, but the plaster job didn't quite match anything else, because we did a horrible job at patching the hole. My dad and I were playing baseball in the house because it was raining outside when I was seven, and I swung my bat back a little too much.

The front windows were replaced twice within a month of each other because my mother wanted new windows and my dad ordered them. A month later, he and I were practicing my pitching, and my curve ball got away from me, smashing into the glass leading to another new large picture window. Mom was pissed, but dad laughed. I missed him.

For anyone who would think I was trying to replace my father with Samuel, they were sorely mistaken. My father was a string bean with thinning gray hair and a slightly hunched posture. And Samuel was the very definition of sexy with his muscles, tats, and beard.

"What are you doing here?"

I jumped when I heard my mother's voice. I'd been so lost in my thoughts, I hadn't noticed she'd emerged from her sick bed looking like crap and holding her stomach. "I heard you were taken by ambulance to the hospital. You should be in bed." She was pale, her hair stringy, and her cheeks were sunken in a little. She'd lost weight.

"Samuel wouldn't have called you. I told him not to," she said, ignoring my comment.

I quirked my eyebrow and tilted my head to the side. Why was it an issue that I came home to check on my ailing mother? "It wasn't him. It was Mrs. Byrd."

"Nosey old woman," she griped harshly in an almost whisper.

"She is, but she thought I should know that an ambulance came and got you yesterday afternoon. Why didn't you call me? Or have Sam call?"

Her brow lifted, wrinkling her forehead. "Since when do you call Mr. Cayden, Sam?"

Her snide tone and demeanor raised my hackles and I wanted to lash out rebelliously, but I tapped it down since she wasn't feeling well. "Since when do you call him by his first name? And besides, it's not like he's my teacher any longer." Okay, I was only able to hold back slightly.

"No, but I'm pretty sure I taught you to respect your elders."

Swallowing my retort, I took in a deep breath and let it out. "What did the doctors say?" I figured her health was probably a safer subject to discuss.

My mother slowly hobbled over to the couch with her shoulders hunched, her body swaying slightly. I tried to help her, but she swatted me away. Seeing her like this, the term "green around the gills" made complete sense to me now.

"They said to rest, drink plenty of fluids, and to take the Tamiflu, but it makes me feel sicker."

"Do you want something to drink?"

"No."

"Mom, Sam said that you were dehydrated. You need to drink something."

She threw her arm over her eyes as she laid back and dragged her feet up onto the couch. She had always been a little dramatic at times, but considering she had the flu, I'd ignore it…even if it was something that got on my nerves about her. "Fine. I think Samuel got some ginger ale. Can you get me some?"

"Sure. What about meds?"

"It's not time yet. I can't take any more of the nausea medicine for another hour."

I left her to carry out her request, and when I returned, I couldn't help but ask, "Mom? Why was Sam, I mean Mr. Cayden, here? Mrs. Byrd said that you two should get married."

She snorted with indignation. "That nosey neighbor needs to shut it. She's been trying to marry me off since a year after your father died and she seems to think anyone will do." It looked like she tried to lift the arm not covering her eyes, but it barely rose, making her appear weaker.

I moved closer and sat on the solid dark wood coffee table in front of her. Before she could say anything, I put the straw I had thrown into the chilled can up to her lips. "Take a drink." She did as I asked, but it was a shallow sip.

Her hand wrapped around the can and she took it away from me. There was a bruise on the back of it, probably from the I.V., but the skin looked more wrinkled and thinner. I could see the tracks of veins crisscrossing under the skin. They appeared more delicate and fragile than I ever remembered them being. I tried to think when she could have possibly aged so much. Had her hands been like that when I left? My eyes drifted to her face. She had more lines and her blue eyes looked a little dull and lifeless. When had her hair changed from an almost honey color to gray? She was only 46.

"That old bat can run off at the mouth and play matchmaker all she wants, but nothing is going to happen. Your father is still the only man I have ever loved or will love. I'm happy with things as they are. As for Samuel, he's been coming by to help me fix up the house."

"Why?" Sure, minor things needed to be fixed, but nothing extensive as far as I knew.

Her eyes shut as if unable to hold my gaze any longer. "I figured with you off at college and it being only me now…I mean, I work in downtown St. Louis and traffic is getting to be a hassle…" She sighed and finally caught my gaze again. "I thought about fixing this place up to sell to get a condo or something closer to the office."

This shocked me. For some reason, I always thought of her and this house being one of the constants in my life. I didn't think about her ever selling it or leaving all the memories of my father behind. I didn't know how to answer her. "Oh," was all I could manage.

"I got a promotion at work, which means I've been working more hours. It's hard to drive almost an hour each way sometimes. They remodeled some of the old buildings in downtown into condos. One of my friends recently moved into them, and I was just thinking it might be nice for me to do the same."

I still didn't know what to say. Granted we hardly spoke, but this was a major decision. I would've thought she'd discuss something of this magnitude with me. I suddenly felt weird and out of place. Betrayal, confusion, and hurt blanketed me, wrapping themselves around me like a second skin. This was my childhood home. The place I grew up in, the place I created memories with my father…and my mother, although those were fewer and further between.

I knew it was selfish of me to expect my mother to stay put, to keep everything the same as it had always been. I knew that. I did, and yet, I still wanted nothing to change. Stupidly, selfishly, I could mature and grow. I could get out of this small town that sat on the edge of St. Louis, but everything about her needed to remain the same. She didn't tell me she was sick, nor that she was fixing up the house to sell. It wasn't fair.

But then again, I never really shared my life with her. My life in school, the men I dated, all of my plans were kept to myself.

I was a horrible son. Sheepishly, I bowed my head and swallowed hard, ashamed of how I felt. "That's great, Mom," I forced out past the lump in my throat. "Do you need anything else?"

She shook her head ever so slightly and grunted.

"Maybe you should go back to bed," I suggested.

Thrusting out the arm closest to me, she felt around with her hand searching for something, her eyes closed tightly. When she tapped my arm, she held it weakly. "Joshy…" I cringed at the sound of the nickname I'd hated since kindergarten. "I was going to tell you, but I'm not even sure I can go through with it. Every time something gets fixed, I feel guilty for even considering selling this place. I say I want to move closer, but the thought of leaving it all behind is scary. Your father and I bought this house right after we got married. I haven't moved in almost thirty years. Lord knows what kind of junk we have hidden in all the nooks and crannies."

That made me feel even shittier. "Mom, it's your life." And it was true, but it didn't stop the resentment churning deep within me. I wondered, if she hadn't gotten sick, if I hadn't been called by Mrs. Byrd, if I hadn't jumped in the car and rushed home, would I have been told about the move after she settled herself into her new place? My father would have spouted some old saying like, "What's good for the goose is good for the gander." I didn't tell her anything about me or my life, she didn't tell me anything about hers, and I was butt hurt that she treated me the same as I did her. Then again, this was a little different since this was about the very house I had been in since my birth.

I lifted my head, noticing her quiet gaze. Her lips curled into a small smile and she sighed. "I'm sorry. I wasn't thinking, but it isn't like you were planning on coming back. As it stands, I haven't seen you in three years."

"You're right." Even saying those words rubbed me raw. After my father died, she threw herself into her work even more so than before. And when she took vacation, she seemed overly busy and never had time to come down and visit me. Of course, I never made time to come back home because I was hiding from Sam.

That made me think of something else. "How did you and Sa—I mean, how did Mr. Cayden start doing all the work?"

"Came to check…"

"Check?" Her eyes were closed and her breathing evened out. She needed to rest, and as much as I debated on waking her up to ask her what she meant, I couldn't do it.

I pulled the throw blanket off the back of the couch and covered her up. Everything was starting to change, but I couldn't figure out what that meant for me.

Once again, my thoughts drifted to Sam. Damn, I still wanted him like I've never wanted anyone else.

***

Samuel

"Have you changed your mind?" My brother Charles's snide voice touched every nerve in my body and made me shudder in phantom pain. As soon as I walked into my house, my phone had started ringing, and without checking the caller id, I answered it. Big mistake.

"Changed my mind? I haven't—as you say—changed my mind. This isn't that I make my mind up and bam, I'm straight," I growled. We'd had this conversation periodically ever since I was thirteen when I told him I liked guys more than girls.

"I would've thought you learned your lesson after that convict."

"Con—? Do you mean Max?" My ex had spent some time in juvenile hall when he was a teen, but when I'd met him, he was working on a doctorate in child psychology. He approached me and our relationship more as a case study than anything else. The guy before that, wanted to experiment with being gay. And the guy before him, believed that sleeping with other people was all part of being true to yourself.

But it was Max who really got into my head and made me question everything about myself. He used me as his little experiment and by the time I got out, I wasn't sure who I was any longer. He was one of the reasons I moved from Los Angeles to Imperial. This small town offered a change of pace, and allowed me to change my life. I welcomed it with open arms.

"Of course him. He was playing you from the start. Then again, given his background, it was a foregone conclusion. Something you should have anticipated. The best thing for you to do is realize your mistake, give up teaching in that podunk little town, and come home where you belong. Marry a nice woman and..." I stopped listening, his words evaporating into nothing.

My brother liked to rub my relationship failures in my face. According to him, two men couldn't love each other nor have a real commitment between them the way a man and woman could. It was impossible since my lifestyle went against everything he believed, and my usual means of dealing with him was to hang up and pray I wouldn't have to talk to him again any time soon.

But today was not normal. Today I had seen the one person I'd been longing to see. The same person I also dreaded running into again. Josh. I still had that letter. After he left, I read it every day. When some time had passed, it became every other day. Now, I pulled it out to read once a week. I forbade myself any more than that.

No, today was anything but normal. The more he talked, the more I wanted to reach through the phone and squeeze my brother's neck. My mother had accepted me, but for whatever reason, my father and brother refused to give me the same courtesy.

In a sense, I essentially did the same thing Josh had done and ran away from home, heading to a college in another state as soon as I could. Of course, our reasons for leaving were different, but I understood the urge to get out and not look back.

"…Father has found you someone he believes will be perfect for you." My ears tuned in again as my brother made that comment. Perfect for me? More like someone he wanted to make a deal with and he thought she would be able to keep me in line.

I laughed darkly, humorlessly. "Unless that person has a cock and balls, not interested."

"Listen—"

"No. I'm sick of your diatribe. Nothing is going to change, nothing has changed in thirty years. I'm gay. I've been gay and will continue to be gay. Nothing you say or do will change that, and if you can't accept it, then do us all a favor and pretend I no longer exist."

Dead silence answered me, and a minute later, I heard the distinct beeping sound of the phone service telling me my call had been disconnected. There was something oddly freeing and painful in that irritating noise.

I dropped the phone on its cradle and shook my head. After all this time, my eyes did not burn with tears, my heart did not yearn for their love. Yes, it hurt because they were my family, however, it was a mere pinprick in the grand scheme of things. Josh held more power to hurt me in the palm of his hands than my own family—not that he realized that. Our lives were on different paths and the likelihood of them crossing forever remained minute.

Or maybe after seeing Josh today, after leaving him the way I had, I was too drained to care about my family's mandates. I could remember after my mother passed away, I tried to live up to my father's expectations. That lasted a total of three weeks, and I couldn't believe I allowed it to go on for that long. They managed to guilt me into trying a relationship with a young lady, and it ended in an epic failure that cost my father a small chunk of change since I "embarrassed the young lady and disgraced her with my proclivities." Never again. I knew who I was and I would never again try to be anything else. You'd think after more than fifteen years, they'd learn.

Walking straight into my kitchen, I yanked my refrigerator door open and grabbed a beer, popping the top off in one smooth motion. I deserved it after the day I'd had. And to my utter disappointment—joy— I'd get to experience it all over again day after day until Josh decided to go back to Florida. My anxiety ramped up at the possibility of seeing him again. At the same time, I couldn't help the anticipation I felt at seeing him again. Both warred for the top emotional spot within me.

Tomorrow.

Josh.

I tipped the bottle of beer back and chugged the whole thing. Tomorrow may very well be the death of me.

Chapter 5

Joshua

Last night after helping my mother get into bed, silence greeted me. Guilt and shame washed over me at how I treated Sam. And it happened all because of Mrs. Byrd and her damn mouth. All I could think about as I sat on the couch in the living room, the television flashing unseen pictures on its screen, was that if I hadn't listened to her, hadn't let her words poison me, I wouldn't have acted as if he was nothing more than an unwanted flea on a dog.

I tried to use the excuse that my feelings were still too raw and too close to the surface—which they were—but even if they hadn't been making my whole body vibrate with lust for him, I still lashed out in jealousy. I'd been jealous of my own mother, afraid she stole him from me. And that right there, was more fucked up than anything else I had ever thought or experienced in my short life.

Sam couldn't be stolen from me, taken away like a toy. He was a man, and he didn't belong to me, even if that was what I desperately wished. And fuck did I wish he was mine.

Maybe it would've been better if I had walked out and driven home after I put my mother in bed, but I couldn't bring myself to leave. I sat on the couch, telling myself that I messed up, however it wasn't only my exhaustion keeping me rooted in this town for the night. For the first time in three years, merely seeing him again made me feel whole and complete. Even when I believed my mother had stolen him from me, he grounded me. It was as if the universe whispered, "This is where you belong."

I passed out staring at the TV at some point while I pondered life and the mess it could make; and when I woke up, I was no closer to figuring out what I wanted than I had been the night before. Correction, I knew what I wanted, but I didn't know how to go about making it happen.

The one thing I realized as I sat there last night stuck in that in-between stage of wakefulness and sleep, was that I wanted Sam. I was no longer an eighteen-year-old kid afraid of what others would say, no longer afraid he didn't want me. And most importantly, I was no longer his student. That ship had sailed a few years ago.

The night before I graduated, I'd finally grown some balls and had written him a letter, which I'd forced him to take from me. It was high time I grew another pair and tried to win him because after all this time, I still loved him. If he turned me away, that was fine, but at least I could say I tried and hadn't allowed this chance to pass me by.

Getting up from the old lumpy couch that was somehow simultaneously the most comfortable and backbreaking thing to sleep on, I schlepped into the kitchen to see if my mother had anything to eat and drink. I hated coffee, preferring instead to down a Mountain Dew or Dr. Pepper while eating something somewhat healthy. It was all about balance. I found fruit, but no Dew. In fact, I found a plethora of food, but I couldn't recall my mother ever having so much healthy stuff in her fridge before. Egg whites, fresh fruits and vegetables, bottles of water sitting next to one of those pitchers with a water filter, and turkey bacon. Turkey bacon! My mother used to say it was fake bacon and she would never buy it.

The world turned upside down. That was the only reason for the contents of the fridge. Maybe I had walked into the wrong kitchen. Possible, but highly unlikely. Still, I turned around and headed straight for the front door intent on verifying the address on the side of the house.

Wrenching the door open, I found Sam standing there wearing a black t-shirt and a pair of navy blue gym shorts looking incredible. I feared drool had begun running down my chin, but it hadn't—thankfully.

"Sam...I mean, Mr. Cayden, what are you doing here?" Way to go, idiot. Can you make yourself look any more foolish? My cheeks burned with embarrassment, and I could feel the heat moving from them through my body, all the way down to my toes.

He cleared his throat, and my eyes locked onto his bobbing Adam's apple. "I came to check on your mother and to see if you needed anything."

I almost shouted, "You," but managed to refrain. "She's still sleeping. I was just about to fix some breakfast. Would you..." I glanced away before meeting his eyes. "Would you like to come in and eat...with me?"

The small smile that appeared on his lips accelerated my pulse and made my heart feel as if it received a jolt. I stood there shifting my weight from foot to foot as I waited for his answer.

"Yeah, sure."

His acceptance thrilled me, but I tried to hide it. I was a 21-year-old man, not a fucking 12-year-old girl with a crush on a boy band.

When he stepped inside, brushing past me, I had to tell myself not to reach out and grab him, not to lean in and breathe in his intoxicating scent. He's here to check on things, that's it. Don't scare him away. My reminder to myself did nothing to slow down my hammering heartbeat or dry my sweaty palms.

For three years, I dreamed of him being in the same room, standing in front of me. Sometimes, I pictured him and me in bed together, and I would grab my cock and stroke it, moving my hand over the tip, using my other hand to reach behind me and slowly finger my hole until I came. Even when I was with other guys, I always imagined Sam, and it was his face in my head every time I blew my load. As much as I tried to forget him, it was impossible.

And now we were in the same house together.

The jealousy and anger I'd experienced yesterday were gone, leaving only a lingering shame at my behavior. I still couldn't believe that I'd been jealous of my mother. Even if she and I didn't have the best relationship, embarrassment made my skin feel hot and my stomach clench.

Jealousy was an emotion I didn't have much experience with. In school, I went through the motions without ever really giving into any feelings, and therefore, I never got jealous of anything my fuck buddies or boyfriends did, which was probably why my relationships didn't last very long. But yesterday, one little suggestion from the nosey next door neighbor, and I was losing my shit. Yeah, I was kind of fucked up.

To make matters worse, I could only stand there gaping at him while he stood feet away from me, unable to take my eyes off of him or to stop their perusal of his body. My mother lay in bed sick with the flu on the other side of the wall as I imagined what it would be like to have Sam throw me against that very wall, pull down my jeans, and thrust into me. Not that it could ever happen like that. Guys were a lot different than girls. We needed lube and stretching. We needed—

The sound of his voice cut through my thoughts. "You okay?" he asked.

If he only knew that being home, being around him made me feel like my feet were firmly planted on solid ground instead of sinking in quicksand. "Yeah, I'm fine."

We stared at each other, uncertainty flowing between us like a set of raging rapids. "Maybe I should go," he finally said hesitantly.

"No! I mean, no, don't. I'm sorry about what I said yesterday. I was upset and—"

"I should've called you."

"What?" I gazed at him in confusion, and then it dawned on me what he meant. "No, that wasn't your fault. My mom can be kind of a tyrant about things and she didn't want me to worry. School is what's important." I'd heard that from her more than once.

"Mr. Cayden—"

"Sam."

"Huh?"

"You can call me Sam. It's not like you're my student any longer."

A smile found its way to my lips. "Sam." His name was a breathless whisper that escaped.

***

Samuel

My name on his lips shot a surge of desire that went straight to my dick. I hadn't been planning on saying that, and I sure as hell hadn't planned on having breakfast with him.

Truth be told, I didn't know what I expected when I hopped in my car and drove over this morning. I hadn't even been sure what I was doing until I pulled up behind Josh's car and threw my car in park. I sat there like a stalker trying to convince myself to either knock on the door or go home. Driving away didn't sound appealing at all. I wanted to see him again, which meant knocking, but at the same time, I was nervous and scared. This was my student—former student—I shouldn't have feelings for him. I shouldn't think about him at all beyond educational purposes, but I did.

If I was the man and educator I was supposed to be, I should've

46

turned around as soon as he opened the door. I couldn't. Instead, I walked inside and agreed to join him for breakfast.

Maybe it was my morbid curiosity about the letter, but honestly, I knew it was more. The letter pulled the blinders off and opened my eyes, and as wrong as it probably was, I wanted him. No, we couldn't have anything lasting. He had a life in Florida, and he deserved more than a high school science teacher that was fourteen years older than him.

Since he'd left, I'd thought about him daily, while he probably forgot me as soon as he stepped foot on campus. Away from this small town, away from his mother and prying eyes, he moved on with his life and realized what he felt for me was not love. Just the mere inkling that that could be true, pained me more than anything my family or exes had done to me. I was pathetic.

"So, uh, breakfast. Eggs and turkey bacon okay? Not sure what happened to my mom while I was gone, but her fridge made me question if I was in a stranger's kitchen." He laughed, but it sounded forced and strained.

"That's fine." I allowed my gaze to drift to the kitchen and then return to him. "She said she wanted to get healthy and asked for some pointers." Confusion marred his face. His brow furrowed and his head tilted to the side. "I don't know why. I wanted to—" I started to add, but stopped abruptly. I almost said something that was better left buried. Showing up unannounced was one thing, helping his mother another, but to admit that I had started helping her in order to keep tabs on him, was pitiful.

He pressed, "Wanted to what?"

"Nothing." I couldn't confess, so I changed the subject. "Did you want help with breakfast?"

His mouth opened to argue, his eyes squinting a little more in irritation, but he didn't continue with his interrogation. "Uh, sure," he mumbled before turning and walking toward the kitchen.

I mentally swiped my brow in relief. I wasn't ready to go there, probably never would be. If I suddenly admitted his letter got to me, that I thought about him daily in a very unteacherlike way, I feared he'd run back to Florida and I'd never see him again. I wanted to take what I could get as long as I could get it.

"If you cook the bacon, I'll deal with the eggs. How do you like them?" he asked.

"Anything is fine."

"Scrambled then. I suck at not breaking the yolk on fried. That okay?"

He seemed nervous, shuffling his weight from side to side, unable to really look me in the eye. Not that I was exactly a statue…okay, I was doing the exact same thing. It was like we were dancing around the elephant in the room and unsure of our steps, our half assed apologies not dealing with the real issue at hand. Maybe we needed dance lessons.

"Yeah, that's fine." Ugh! My words came out almost robotic in nature. "I—"

At the same time I started, he said, "Hey—"

An awkward moment of the highest caliber.

"Go ahead," I encouraged him, although I wasn't sure I wanted to hear what he had to say after yesterday. The argument was still fresh in my mind, causing my stomach to flip and tighten up in knots. My chest constricted, making it hard to breathe, and still I waited for the guillotine to fall.

"I shouldn't have flown off the handle yesterday. I was just…" he began.

I stood there like a statue, my lungs burning from not releasing the air I had trapped in them. When he didn't continue, I prodded, "Yes?"

He shrugged, but his chin practically rested on his chest so that I couldn't see his face. Without answering, he spun around and pulled out the bacon and eggs from the refrigerator, setting them gently on the counter. With his back turned, I heard his soft reply. "I didn't want to lose."

What did that mean? I wasn't trying to come between him and his mother. I would never do that. Granted, their relationship left something to be desired—not that I was an expert by any means—but she was still his parent, and the only one he had left. "You aren't going to lose your mom. I wasn't trying—"

Whirling around, his glare could melt the polar ice caps. "What do you mean?"

Instinctively, I took a step backward.

"Is there something going on with my mother?" He spat the last word as if it left a foul taste in his mouth.

"No," I spoke quickly. She would be one of the last people on earth

I would think about in any sense other than as his mother.

"Then what do you mean?" he demanded.

Fire and ice. One minute there was an unspoken awkward gap between us, and the next the chasm opened and the switch was flipped. He went from hesitant to furious before I batted an eye, and I was having a hard time keeping up. His chest heaved with the deep breaths he was taking and his face, which had a slight flush to it, turned red. His jaw was clenched and his hands were fisted.

"What exactly are your intentions toward my mother?" he sneered.

His anger began to feed my own. How dare he accuse me of anything when he hadn't a single goddamn clue? Marching up to him, I pushed him against the counter behind him, accidentally knocking off the carton of eggs, and they fell to the floor. "You don't know anything," I growled right before I crashed my lips against his in a brutal kiss. His hands fisted in my shirt, and I couldn't tell if he was trying to push me away or pull me closer. I prayed for the latter.

Both of my hands were gripping his hips tightly. I moved one to his face, using my fingers to put pressure on his chin, opening his mouth for a heavier onslaught. My tongue plunged in, snaking around his, tasting him.

His tongue wrestled with mine for control. It was an aphrodisiac.

And then a bird squawked, a car alarm blared…our bubble was broken.

I let him go quickly, stumbling backward with wide eyes and a racing heart. His eyes were also wide with shock, and his mouth looked red and raw from my beard. He had been thoroughly kissed and I craved more of him. Instead of going to him though, I apologized, "Sorry," and then hightailed it out of the house. I couldn't believe I'd done that.

Jumping into my car, I ran away like Josh had done multiple times. For me though, I was pretty sure if I hadn't left, he would have kicked me out.

***

Joshua

What the fuck just happened? Had I dreamed that? Sam kissed me. I couldn't believe it. Sam really kissed me.

Slowly, I brought my hand to my face and felt the skin around my mouth that had been scraped by his beard, and I could feel the smile curling my lips upward. He'd kissed me, and as soon as I felt his lips press against mine, the sky opened up and I heard the angels singing. Well, maybe not that dramatic, but something like that. The ground beneath me shifted and my life, my whole world, came into complete focus.

Kissing him, his arms gripping me, had filled a void within me. The same void that had opened up the day I laid eyes on Sam. I'd tried to fill that space with others, and when I couldn't, a couple of fuck buddies helped to distract me and scratch an itch. But two minutes with him did what no one else could do. I felt whole.

At least until the moment he left me standing in the kitchen alone and reeling from the best kiss I'd ever experienced.

A new determination burned within me. Samuel Cayden would be mine. I'd find a way to win him and prove that no one else could ever compare.

Chapter 6

Joshua

The only time I heard from Sam over the past two days was when he called to check on my mother. He never stayed on the phone for very long, and it had started to piss me off. He mentioned nothing about our kiss or his leaving, and the only thing he would ever discuss was my sick mother. I tried my best not to be jealous, but it was hard not to when he focused on her alone.

On top of that, he never came by. Coward. Funny, I'd used that word on myself, but to me, things were different now. I knew what I wanted, and I was done running. It sounded well and good, however, if he didn't cooperate, I couldn't exactly succeed or enact my dastardly plan.

My frustration grew, and I was at a loss as to what to do. Five minutes ago when he called, I tried to bring up what happened in the kitchen, and he said, "Sorry, I have to go." He hung up without another word. His lack of cooperation made everything difficult.

Slamming down the house phone after he hung up, I huffed in frustration, and picked it up again to call him back and rip him a new one. However, before I pressed any of the numbers, my mother wandered out of her bedroom. She'd been in bed for the past couple of days without getting up much, fighting the flu and her fever. Today, she finally had a little color in her pale cheeks. Some said I took after her more than my father. In the face, I had to agree. I had her coloring—our skin could tan easily, giving us a healthy glow–her delicate smile—something I cringed about whenever someone mentioned it—and her rich mahogany hair with a few blonde and red strands woven in. But the eyes that stared back at me in the mirror were not my mother's gray eyes, they were my father's chocolate browns. Something that made me both miss him and feel like he was there, watching over me.

Rushing to her side, I helped her to the couch and asked, "How are you feeling?"

"Better, but as much as I love that room, I'm this close to going stir crazy in it." She held up her fingers, holding them about an inch apart. Her breathing came out erratic, like she had just run a marathon instead of walked the short distance from her bedroom to the couch.

I felt her forehead. No fever. "Do you need anything?"

"I need you to go back to school and finish the semester. I know you're in the middle of finals."

"Nope."

"Joshy—"

"Mom." I cut her off using the same tone she was using on me. "I'm actually done. My grades were high enough that I was exempt from a couple of them, and the ones I did have to take, I finished the day I got the call. I'm done with the semester."

"Oh." Her voice dripped with disappointment as she stared out the large picture window. "What about your internship? Weren't you supposed to be going out on a boat or something to study dolphins?"

"Sharks and a few other things, and it doesn't start for a couple of weeks."

"Then shouldn't you go so that you can get ready for that?"

"Why are you trying to get rid of me?" I demanded. We hadn't seen each other in almost three years, and she seemed awfully insistent on getting me out the door.

"I'm not." She still didn't look at me and continued to stare out the window.

I couldn't help but wonder if I had missed something, but for the life of me, I couldn't begin to fathom what it was.

"Mom."

She sighed. "Joshy, your life is in Florida now. The sooner you head back, the sooner you can get back to it. It's not that I don't love seeing you. I do, however, you can't actually tell me that you want to be here. You couldn't get out of here fast enough after graduation, and didn't consider coming back until that damn nosey Mrs. Byrd called you to tell you about the ambulance. Imperial was always too small for you. It's best if you go home."

Home. For some reason that word didn't bring to mind Florida. It made me think of this little house where I was raised, where my parents loved me and each other, and it brought to mind Sam and the way he held me.

"I think I'll stay a few more days to make sure you're all right. I'm not missing anything by being here," I commented, trying to keep my words and tone light, almost flippant. If I went back to Tallahassee now, I had a feeling that I'd miss something big. And if I left, my chances with Sam would go up in flames, ending everything before it even had a chance to begin.

"Joshy, you don't have to. I'm fine," she stressed.

My curiosity climbed. "I know you will be, but you still look like death warmed over." I didn't want to be insistent, but I wasn't going anywhere. Besides, when I finally decided to head south, Florida would still be there waiting for me.

"Listen…"

I anxiously waited for her to continue. My body broke out in a cold sweat, and my jaw clenched tightly. This conversation had put my body on edge, ready to spring at an enemy, although I didn't know who or what my adversary was.

It took her a minute of sitting there not paying any attention to me before she finally turned her head and met my gaze straight on. "Samuel isn't the man for you." Her words were clipped and harsh.

My head spinning, I wanted to know where that had come from. Opening my mouth, I closed it with a snap and ground my teeth together with such force, it'd be a miracle if I still had any after this. The only people I'd told about my feelings were my father and Sam, but given the way I'd acted the day before, it wouldn't surprise me if she had figured it out for herself. Still, that didn't give her the right to dictate my love life. "Why did you say that?"

"Joshy, I know you've decided you're gay, and I accept it, but he isn't the man for you." She repeated her statement, but it was her words before that which grabbed my attention. I'd decided? She accepted it?

When I came out to my parents, I chose my father to hear it first. I was fifteen. My mother had been trying to get me to take out some girl who was a daughter of someone she worked with. I kept refusing, eventually telling my dad why I couldn't go through with it. I'd known I was attracted to guys over girls for a long time, but never admitted it aloud until I talked to my dad. I remembered him patting me on the shoulder before pulling me in for a hug. He loved me no matter whom I chose to love. That was true acceptance.

He told me he would deal with my mother. That night—it was a Friday because my mother was actually home the next day, not that it always happened like that, but it was always something that stuck out to me—there was a lot of yelling, and the next morning, I came out of my basement bedroom and found the table set with a huge breakfast. My mother was the one manning the stove and my father was nowhere in sight. She had the audacity to tell me I was confused and that I just needed to date a girl to realize I'd been wrong.

It took time, but she finally backed off and when it came to my love life, she pretended it didn't exist, choosing instead to ignore it. Accepted? That's not acceptance—unless she came to some sort of epiphany since I'd been gone. I couldn't hide my shock and slight disdain when I said, "You accepted it? You can actually say that with a straight face right after you claimed it was my decision? And why do you think Sam isn't for me?"

"Mr. Cayden!" she snapped.

"Sam," I sneered. "He told me I could call him that, ergo, I will."

"I see you've forgotten your manners while in college. What do they teach you down there?" Her mumbled words were made toward the window.

"They teach me that respect is earned and not just given, and they teach me what mutual respect is. I haven't forgotten my manners. You're the one that taught me if someone gives you permission to call them by their first name, you can if it isn't a formal situation. So, I think I'll call him Sam since he said I could."

"Watch your attitude!"

"My attitude? You're the one who started to attack me. Funny, a couple of days ago, you were fine with him, but now you want to what? Keep us apart? Newsflash, we aren't together."

"I saw you! I saw you two in the kitchen kissing," she yelled, her breathing heavy and labored.

"So?"

"He's your teacher!"

"Former teacher. Here's something else you may not know, I've loved him since I was in high school. I told dad and he told me to wait until I graduated before saying anything. I did that. I wrote Sam a letter and then hopped in my car and drove to Florida. I'm twenty-one, you can't tell me what I can and can't do. You can't tell me who I can and can't…date." I almost said fuck, but changed it. "I'm gay. Accept it because you can't change it. I used to think that you would finally get off your high horse, but I'm guessing that hasn't happened yet. When I was fifteen, you told me it was wrong and went against the bible. Funny, you weren't overly religious before that. Your family, yes, but not you. Or was it that you were more afraid of what everyone would think? I know we live in what feels like the Catholic capital of the USA, but that doesn't mean I can't be who I am. I will not change for you or anyone else."

"He's older than you."

If she thought that argument was going to work, she was sadly mistaken. "Dad was older than you by twelve years. Sam is only fourteen years older than me."

"You're still a child."

"No, I'm not. I'm old enough to vote, drink legally, and to be drafted. I live on my own and pay my own bills. The only thing you pay for is my school and part of my rent since I don't live in the dorm any longer, but even that I pay half of. What part of that sounds like a child?" This hadn't been the conversation I planned on having today, or ever, with anyone. My whole body tingled and felt hot, and my teeth gnashed against each other as my jaw moved back and forth. "And you want to talk age? You and dad started to date when you were only 17. So do you really want to have this conversation? Is it that Sam is older, or that he's a guy?"

"You shouldn't talk to your mother that way."

"And you should probably learn to accept that your son is gay and he will always be gay!" I screamed. Seething, I ran down to the basement, slamming my door behind me. Maybe that had been a little childish, but right now, I didn't care, and my little "talk" with my mother didn't change anything. I loved Sam and I was old enough to make my own decisions.

***

Samuel

Every time I heard Josh's voice over the phone, I almost gave into my desire and ran over to his house to throw him over my shoulder and drop him on the closest bed, but instead my conscience held me by a tight leash. I ignored the part of me that demanded I claim him, and instead I hid, punishing myself with the brief chats about his mother. God, I was a fucking idiot.

Too many thoughts swirled in my head. He's too young. He has a life in Florida. Why would he want you, when he could be with someone younger and better?

Normally, my self-esteem was through the roof. At thirty-five, at I had a great body that I took care of, worked out, and my ink drew attention en masse. But Josh had the power to sweep the rug out from under me, which made me second guess everything. With him, normal flew away with the wind and it didn't take anything more than a small breeze.

And I wanted him. One taste and I became addicted. My self-esteem aside, my biggest issue with everything was that he had been a student of mine. How would it look? What would people say or think? In this small town, people would start talking sooner rather than later, and they could be brutal. For that matter, they'd even spread the gossip and whisper in the corners twenty minutes down the road in St. Louis. Sometimes, even the big city had a small town mentality, and anything this Catholic Bible belt didn't agree with, they made known.

I'd never hidden who I was or my sexual preferences, but when I got the job, the superintendent of the school strongly suggested I not discuss it. Then he told me, if I needed to "get my jollies"—his words—I go as far away from Imperial as possible. Some of my friends wondered why I stayed. Sometimes I wondered that myself, but truthfully, the kids were good and it got me away from my family. As long as I kept my nose clean and did my job, no one could say anything.

Besides, after being in California since I was a kid, I liked the idea of living in a small town where the pace of life was slower and more relaxed. It took me years to make the decision to leave Cali and move far away from my family, but I finally did it and never regretted my decision or anything else. Not even my feelings for Josh. Scared, yes, but I didn't regret them. That said, I still believed he could do better than me…someone closer to his own age, and someone who didn't have his family trying to marry him off to some random woman.

I'd told my brother to lose my number, but that little shit was persistent. I didn't how to make him or my father see reason. Maybe if I got married to some random guy they'd finally understand. But the only man that ever came to mind was Josh, and I wouldn't do that to him. Maybe I could fake my own death, live out in the wilderness, and off their radar. I knew what plants I could eat and the ones I couldn't, and Missouri had enough forest area that I could easily get lost and never be found.

It was funny what your mind concocted when you were frustrated.

Simply thinking about my family stirred up my irritation and frustration. I scratched my chest and easily pictured punching them both.

My phone rang, and I almost felt bad for the person who called me, until she opened her mouth.

"Samuel?"

"Alice? Are you okay? Something you or Josh need?" Saying his name gave me a small thrill, and my hand instinctively went to my lips as if I could still feel his soft mouth on mine.

"Stay away from my son."

Excuse me? That wasn't what I'd expected when I picked up the phone. My displeasure with my family began to encompass her. "I'm sorry? What do you mean?"

"I saw you kissing him."

"Alice…" How was I supposed to respond to that? I had kissed him and I still wanted to kiss him.

"He's a good boy, and he has a bright future. He doesn't need you corrupting him."

Corrupting him. My irritation began to morph into anger and I hit my head with the palm of my hand. "I completely agree. He is a bright young man and has a lot going for him, which is why I wrote him a recommendation letter to FSU. As for the corrupting, I have no idea what you're talking about."

"I didn't realize you were gay," she mumbled under her breath, but I heard it.

"Always have been, and always will be."

"Stay away from him."

I should've agreed, but instead I opened my mouth and allowed whatever words that wanted to break free, to do so. "First of all, whether I'm around him or not won't change the fact that he is a good guy with a future. Secondly, he's an adult now, and he can make his own decisions about who he wants to be with. Third, you should open your eyes and learn a little something about him. He's strong-willed, brilliant, a great friend, and dependable. In high school, people turned to him when they needed a friend, a laugh, and support. He gave it all freely, even after your husband died. I have no doubt that he's very much the same in college, but I'm willing to bet money, you didn't know that about him."

"Don't tell me who you think my son is—"

"I don't think, I know," I cut in. "You're the one who thinks you know Josh, but you don't. You never came to any meetings in school, and when I called you concerning him, you blew me off and basically told me to mind my own business. So excuse me if I don't put much stock into what you think you know, or don't know, about your son. I will say that I didn't know he was gay until after he graduated, and the first communication I've had with him is when he showed up to check on you. He showed up for you, which means he loves you. I don't think I know things about your son, I know them as fact because I coached him in baseball, tutored him when he got behind, and was there for him when he needed someone and had nothing more to give the people around him. When his father..." I stopped short, forcing myself to shut up before I said something I shouldn't. Although, I might have gone further with my chastisement than I had initially thought I would, but she deserved it.

A soft gasp and sniffle came through the line. I was an ass and made a woman cry. My mother was probably watching me from Heaven and rolling her eyes ready to smack the back of my head. I sighed. "I'm sorry for berating you, but Josh is a good guy and is no longer a kid." I refused to give into her completely. Something about agreeing to stay away from Josh didn't sit well with me, even if I believed it might be the right thing to do.

"Does this mean you won't stay away from him?" she whimpered.

"That's up to him. It's his decision to make." I couldn't believe I had said that, but what had happened in that kitchen was between Josh and me. I hadn't brought his mother in for a fucking threesome.

"I see. And that's your final answer?"

"Yes."

"And if I threaten your job?"

I hissed. "Anything that's happened between us, has happened since he's been back to check on you, and a serious accusation like that would take proof."

"Yes, but it would ruin your reputation."

Suddenly, I heard Josh in the background. "Are you threatening Sam?"

"This doesn't concern you." Her voice suddenly sounded muffled as if she covered the phone.

"I can't believe you. Well, if you want to punish someone, you should know that I'm the one who threw myself at him. I'm the one that fell in love with him and told him the night of my graduation, and I'm the one who forced him to kiss me," Josh declared.

"No, you were led astray—"

"Oh, Mother. Listen to yourself. Guess what? I'm gay and that isn't going to change. Sam isn't the one who turned me gay. And here's another news flash, I've fucked or been fucked by at least ten different guys since I've been in college."

The line went dead.

Ten different guys. I shouldn't be hurt or surprised, but I was. College was a time to discover yourself, to experiment, and he had apparently done just that. I expected him to, but hearing exactly how many men he'd been with bothered me.

Josh spouted his love, and then left to experience everything college life had to offer, and I was here feeling betrayed. I could hear my brother's voice saying gay men couldn't be loyal to just one, but that was bullshit and I knew it. It didn't matter what genders were involved in a relationship. Where was it written that a man could only be loyal to a woman? Relationships took work, but Josh and I weren't in a relationship. He could sleep with whomever he chose. Period.

At least, I told myself that I should be all right with it. In reality, I didn't want to think about him with other men. I was fucked up. I didn't want him with others, I ran away from him, and then I refused to tell his mother I wouldn't have anything to do with him. I was worse than some of my indecisive students.

It also made me a hypocrite. Unable to forget him, I tried to drown his memory by going out or sleeping with other men, but it failed. I finally gave up, deciding I would move on when I quit thinking about him. I hadn't been out with anyone else for a year.

When I finally thought I was on the verge of moving on, Josh showed up out of the blue and I found myself back at square one. And now this new information…I didn't know how to process it all. Maybe I could get drunk and have my own fuck fest. Unfortunately for me, that wasn't who I was, and I'd never been someone who jumped from bed to bed.

I also had to worry about my job. I didn't know if I should be afraid that Alice would follow through with her threats, or if she was simply using them as a scare tactic. I loved my job and didn't want to lose it. I hated when people tried to paint me into a corner. It didn't work with my family, and I'd be damned if I caved to her.

I walked down the hall off of the dining room and pushed my bedroom door open. Light blue walls with white, gauze curtains, and tan furniture greeted me. This room was peaceful and serene, and made me think of the ocean, which ultimately led to thoughts of Josh.

Plopping down on the side of the bed, I pulled open the letter Josh had written me what seemed like a lifetime ago. It was worn and had started to separate where it'd been folded and refolded by me. I no longer needed to read it to know what it said; I had it memorized. My eyes scanned it anyway and found his declaration. I didn't know if I trusted this confession any longer, or if I should chalk it up to schoolboy infatuation. It shouldn't matter, and yet, it did.

I was too old, his ex-teacher, and he'd moved on without me. Add to that his mother's threats, and I should want to tuck tail and run. But I didn't. I stood my ground, still unable to completely let go of him.

Chapter 7

Joshua

She had no right. No right to threaten Sam. Once again, my mother thought more about appearance than me or anyone else. After she'd hung up the phone, we yelled and fought until she succumbed to the flu. Swaying slightly, she fell on the couch in a boneless heap. I couldn't bring myself to feel sympathy for her. I was too angry and upset.

Even after she collapsed onto the couch, I screamed, "Why the hell did you do that? Why don't you leave me and my love life alone?" It was wrong. She was sick and I couldn't have cared less; I just kept attacking her.

"Stop," she mumbled weakly.

I didn't. "Do you want to know everything? I saw him and had a crush. That crush turned into more. And then after Dad died, Sam was the person who was there for me and helped me cope. God knows it sure as hell wasn't you."

My mother tried to narrow her eyes and wound up covering them with her hands. "I was grieving too." Her body shook with tremors and I heard the distinct sound of a small whimper.

It knocked the wind out of my sails, and I plopped down onto the coffee table in front of her. "Sorry for yelling." I wasn't apologizing for being angry, especially after the discussion she and I already had, but this discussion could've waited for a time when she felt better.

She fell back and rested her head on the cushiony back of the couch, her arm covering her eyes. "He's not for you," she stated weakly. She started to gulp in air.

"That's for us to decide, not you."

"You need to find a good gir—"

"That won't ever happen."

She sighed, almost sounding resigned. "Then you need to find someone closer to your age."

"You and dad—"

"And you see how that turned out," she snapped before moaning and grabbing her stomach.

I was clueless about her meaning. "He loved you until the day he died."

"Exactly! And he's gone."

Someone could have broken into the house at that moment, and I wouldn't have noticed.

Breathing heavily, she spoke. "It's not right for a teacher to date his student." She held up her hand before I could argue and cut me off. "It's not, and I think you need to go back to Florida as soon as possible so that you're out of his reach and influence. But more than that, you need to be with someone your own age because if you're not, you could lose her too soon."

I wanted to slap her for once again saying "her," but I'd ignore that for now. The other part wasn't so easily forgotten. "Are you saying that your time with Dad was a mistake?"

"No, I…" She lay in silence for a moment before she said, "I'm tired. I think I'm going to go back to bed. Can you help me up?"

I grabbed her arm and easily lifted her from the couch. Had she always been that light? I'd lifted her with ease.

She left me standing there without another word and when she got to her room, I heard the soft click of her closing the door.

The way she left things got me thinking. Did she regret marrying my father? Was it because I couldn't be everything she believed I should be? I wasn't exactly what she imagined for a son, and she didn't appreciate the fact I liked men over women, but surely that wouldn't be enough for her to rethink her life choices.

When I'd come upstairs earlier, I'd had every intention of going over to Sam's house to talk to him until I heard her threats. She infuriated me, and I squeezed my car keys in my palm, hissing when I realized I almost cut myself. Shoving them into my pocket, I fisted my hands at my side and stormed to her side, demanding answers.

Reaching into my jeans now, I found them again. I could go over there and talk to him, or I could run away again. It wouldn't take much to grab my stuff and return to Florida, to listen to my mother, essentially forgetting about Sam, but I'd run too often and too much. It was time to stop and step forward into whatever future I chose for myself. I knew in the end, someone would not be happy with my choice, and that was something I could live with.

***

An hour later, I sat outside Sam's house on the opposite side of the highway, the newer side. It hadn't changed since the last time I saw it. It still had the gray siding and the small porch hardly big enough for two people to stand on. It still had one white column which looked like someone's poor attempt to replicate a Roman column in the corner before the little alcove. On one side sat the wall of the garage, and on the other there was about two feet where the house extended beyond the door.

The bright green door stood out against the drabness of the exterior, but it worked. He told me that he loved the color green because it reminded him of spring and summer, his two favorite seasons because of baseball. Luckily, even though he came from the west coast, he was still a Cardinals' fan. Perfect taste in professional teams—not that it was a deal breaker if he wasn't.

The bushes in front of his house had grown taller than the windows they sat under. Not the whole bush, but a couple of stragglers had grown taller than the rest of the greenery, and everything was in bloom with white flowers. If I rolled down the windows and breathed deeply, I'd probably smell them. A couple of weeks before I started my senior year, we had tackled yard work here and he tried to uproot the bushes, but the task had been too great a job and he decided it was easier to leave them than to call someone else to pull them out. Now as I sat there and looked at it all, I grinned goofily at the memory.

When I left my mom's house, I'd gotten in my car and started driving, unsure of where I was going. I needed to think, and before I knew it, I was sitting out front staring at the house I had only been to a handful of times. It seemed as if I did that a lot here, started in one direction only to end up in a place that held good memories of days gone by.

I also took that as the answer to my question. Of course, I pretty much already knew I'd chosen him. I hadn't been able to move on or

63

forget him, and that kiss…I wanted those every day for the rest of my life. At fifteen, I saw the man I wanted to spend the rest of my life with, and at twenty-one, I was finally going to grab him with both hands and hold on.

Opening the car door, I exhaled slowly and started up the driveway, brushing my fingers along his car as I strolled by it toward the walkway that led to the front door. One step up to the small porch, and my finger pressed the doorbell.

My heart raced, my hands tingled as if they had been asleep and were just waking up, and I was sweating more from the nerves and less from the warm temperature. I was pretty sure if I lifted my arm and looked, I would find a huge wet stain covering my t-shirt under my pits, growing larger with every passing second. My breathing was coming out in short gasps, making my head feel light and dizzy.

And when the door finally opened, my breath left me in a rush and I fell to the side, throwing myself against the wall of the garage.

"Josh," Sam exclaimed as he rushed over to me.

So uncool. Pathetic really. I came here to talk to him, to convince him that we belonged together, and I managed to hyperventilate on his porch before he could open the door.

I laughed. Still unable to breathe, I began laughing, but it came out sounding more like a wounded seal since I never managed to catch my breath. Lifting my head slightly, I saw the worried expression on Sam's face. His eyes were wide and he reminded me of my roommate anytime I did something stupid—I was quite familiar with the expression.

I gulped in air and tried to stop laughing, but it didn't work and before I knew it, a strong hand grabbed the back of my neck and pushed me forward, bending me in half. With my body in that position, I found it nearly impossible to laugh. I started to breathe normally. Better.

"Are you done being the Joker, or did you want to try for another round?" he asked me, and I heard the hint of humor in his voice.

Taking the chance, I peered up at him. The lines of worry that had marred his face had disappeared and a small smile appeared. My gaze returned to the ground before I answered, "I'm good."

His grip on my neck disappeared. It hadn't been the most comfortable experience, but I already missed his touch. Slowly, I stood up straight, my body still leaning against the vinyl siding that covered the outside of his house.

"You sure you're okay?" He sounded unsure.

"Yeah. I'm fine." My eyes finally met his. He wasn't taller than me, however, when it came to muscle mass, I looked scrawny compared to him. "You okay?" I wasn't sure why I asked, but I wanted to know where I stood with him. I needed to know if my mother succeeded in terrifying him enough that he chose to sever ties with me.

His eyes swept over my body. "Yeah. What are you doing here?"

"I came to talk."

"Maybe it would be—"

"No. Do not finish that sentence."

"Josh."

"Sam." I noticed that when I called him by his name, he closed his eyes. His expression reminded me of someone savoring a bite of something they loved. If it got me what I wanted, I'd use it. "Sam, I only came to talk."

He sighed heavily and finally relented. "Come inside."

Sam led the way in and when I crossed the threshold, I saw that nothing had changed in here either. To the left from the entry way was his office and two bedrooms. Past the living room and to the left, lay his bedroom. Beyond the living room, I could see the green kitchen. He swore he painted it that color so that no one would be able to see the mess on the walls. It was a dark evergreen color, so that may be true, but I believed it had more to do with the fact that green was his favorite color.

The TV hung high on the royal blue accent wall with the couch on the opposite wall with two windows on either side of it. Other than that, he had a coffee table, a love seat and a recliner. No dining room table or big entertainment center. He had a couple of egg crates where his DVR and Blu-ray player sat. He claimed they worked just fine, and since his TV wasn't sitting on it, I supposed he was right. However, I couldn't pass on the opportunity to tease him about it. "I see you still haven't bought any adult furniture."

"I have a couch, that's adult enough."

I was alone with him in his house. I wanted him to think I was "adult enough" too. My heart sped up, and I swallowed hard. Suddenly, I was afraid he heard it and my eyes darted to his. I swallowed again. "Yeah, I guess it is." My palms started to sweat as much as my pits.

He crossed his arms over his chest, pulling his t-shirt tight, outlining his muscles to the point I could probably paint their definition without him removing a stitch of clothing. I hoped I hadn't began drooling.

"What did you want to talk about?"

"What…?" I had to get a grip. "I wanted…I wanted to talk to you about the kiss the other day."

His cheeks started to turn pink under his beard as he dropped his gaze from mine and cleared his throat. He shifted from foot to foot, running a hand through his hair. "What about it?"

"Why did you kiss me?"

***

Samuel

If I expected him to drop it, I'd been sorely mistaken. I somehow knew he wouldn't. My stomach flipped and my nerves ignited, making me feel hot and my skin buzzed with sensation. My shirt began to feel scratchy.

Unable to hold his gaze after he brought up the kiss, I didn't know how to look him in the eye. That was going to come up eventually. I'd thought about my answer, about what I wanted to tell him. I even rehearsed my damn speech. Only now that he was standing here in my space, everything I'd practiced over the last couple of days had disappeared.

"Sam." My name on his lips wrapped around me like a gentle breeze on a summer's day, and at the same time sounded more erotic than anything else I'd ever experienced.

I closed my eyes and swayed backward. That word had power over me.

"Sam," he said again, this time more insistently.

His eyes were a little wide, his kissable mouth slightly open; he didn't appear to be breathing. Maybe he was as nervous as I was.

"I kissed you because I wanted to." The truth poured from my lips.

"Why?"

Persistent shit. My muscles were rigid, but I couldn't stand still. Pacing heavily, I finally threw my hands in the air. "I did it…" Words caught in my throat from fear of how Josh would react.

"Because why?" He reminded me of a kid who constantly asked "why", except he wasn't a kid. He'd grown up a lot since he'd left.

I met his eyes and opened myself up to him. "Because since you left I've thought about you non-stop, because you managed to do what no one else has been able to do, and because I want you."

His mouth fell open and he gasped. He took a couple of tentative steps toward me. His voice was soft and shaky when he spoke. "What have I managed to do?"

In a whisper, I replied, "Captured my attention and made me feel things for you I've never felt for another person."

His feet carried him to where I stood. We were mere inches away, and I could feel the heat radiating from his body. I should tell him to leave, that his mother was right. I should question his reasoning for being here like he questioned me about the kiss, and yet, the words would not form. I should tell him that he belonged with someone his own age, maybe one of the ten guys he's been with in college. I should, but I didn't. I couldn't.

My heart thundered. I could hear my pulse pounding in my ears. Now that I'd confessed, my knees buckled, making me stumble and take a step backward away from him, barely managing to remain upright. I'd been holding that secret for years, and now that it was out, I was nervous.

Josh didn't let me go. He took a step forward, his body eating up the space I'd left, and reached out. Placing a hand over my heart, I was sure he could feel the thumping, telling him exactly how I felt. He slid his other arm around my neck, bringing me in so close that I could feel the warmth of his breath on my face. I let go of my anger and uncertainty. Instead, I wrapped my arms around his waist.

Our lips found each other, and I held us closer together, with no space between us. If I thought the last kiss had been spectacular, then this one was out of this world.

His tongue licked my lips and I opened for him. He didn't wait, his tongue plunged in and I sucked on it. Much like the last time, everything about him was an aphrodisiac that made me want more of him. It was like he cast a spell, and I did not want the magic to disappear.

Josh pulled my hair and a moan rumbled from his chest. My dick got harder—if that was even possible. I was half-hard the moment I opened the door and found him breathing erratically on my doorstep. Maybe it made me cocky, but the mere thought that I could incite that kind of reaction was heady.

My hands slid down his waist and I squeezed his ass, grinding against him. His erection was just as hard as mine. I groaned in pleasure. Nothing I'd experienced before now had ever felt like this. Everything with Josh was hotter, more pleasurable…just more.

Our kiss broke and my lips moved to his jaw, giving him little nips and bites. He tilted his head to give me better access. "Sam," he breathlessly whimpered.

I knew this was wrong and that I shouldn't be doing this, but fuck it all. This was my chance, and if the bubble was going to burst in a few days when Josh headed south again, then I would take what I could get now. Maybe this was what we both needed to move on.

Nipping at his neck, I smiled against him when he sucked in a deep breath, his hands grabbing my head, directing it where he wanted it to go. I sucked hard where his neck met his shoulder, leaving a small imprint, a reminder for later that I had been there. His hands gripped me harder, his short nails digging into my scalp. I marked him. He was mine. For as long as he was home, he was mine.

I reached for his face, knocking his arms off of my head, and they automatically found their way to my hips, his fingers dipping into the waistband of my jeans. My lips crashed against his again. It was pure and raw, and I never knew a kiss could be like this. The lovers from my past, only served a purpose to piss off my father. No one compared to the young man in my arms.

"Sam, more," he groaned when I released his lips momentarily. His hands were tugging on my t-shirt.

Smirking, I gave into his silent request and lifted my shirt over my head, throwing it on the loveseat beside me. "You too," I ordered, and he wasted no time in removing his own shirt. Lines had been branded onto his skin from the Florida sun, giving him a sexy farmer's tan. I could easily picture him in a wetsuit swimming the ocean, only the parts not covered being colored by the rays of the sun.

His grin looked almost mischievous. It curled up more on one side than the other. Josh leaned forward and whispered, "More." That one word went straight to my dick and I swore it jumped in anticipation.

My hands grabbed his hips and started to push him toward the bedroom. Regardless of what happened, the couch was not the best place to continue this sort of fun. Maybe another time…if there was another time.

I wasn't sure if he noticed a change in my countenance or simply felt like kissing me, but before I could lose myself in my own head, his lips were on mine and I was blindly guiding him toward my bedroom, all thoughts of what tomorrow or the future would bring forgotten and buried.

Once we reached my room, my hands went to the fly of his jeans and unbuttoned them. Something about button fly jeans was fucking sexy. Hell, anything Josh wore would probably make me pant like a thirsty man in a desert.

His hands fumbled their way to my own fly, and our arms started to get tangled. We were anxious, our nerves were frayed, and we were stumbling slightly, trying to find our way around each other, but I didn't care and I had a feeling he didn't either. He attacked my jeans, determined to get them unbuttoned and the zipper down, and as soon as he did, his hand dove in, wrapping around my length, which ached to be released from my briefs.

I pushed his jeans over the curve of his ass and squeezed, my fingers slipping between his globes ever so slightly. I wanted to fuck him, to bury myself in his tight hole. Snarling with desire, I pushed him on the bed and pulled his pants off in one yank, my breath hitching when I realized he was commando. "Josh." My voice was reverent.

His smile almost mocked me—almost—but he couldn't deny his own desire when I saw the pre-cum leaking onto his stomach from his dick. He was needy for attention. So I gave him what he wanted, what he really came here for.

I pulled his legs to the end of the bed and fell to my knees, his cock was right in front of my face and I wanted a taste. I grabbed his dick, squeezing him in my fist. His answering cry and the way his hips thrust upward told me how much he enjoyed it. My lips curled into another smirk. I leaned forward and stuck the tip of my tongue out to taste the pre-cum that leaked from the crown of his cock, watching as a thin line dangled between my mouth and his dick.

"Sam, please," Josh begged.

Giving in, I engulfed his length until it reached the back of my throat. I didn't have much of a gag reflex, but he wasn't exactly small. It had been a while since I'd given anyone a blow job, and it was going to take a little work for me to take his full length. Drawing back, I hollowed out my cheeks and sucked hard before sinking down on him a little further than before. I moved my head slowly, glancing up at him through hooded eyes, and from my vantage point, I could see that he teetered on the brink of insanity. Just when I thought I had the upper hand, his hand sank into my hair to keep my head in place, while his hips jerked upward, and he started to fuck my face.

"Oh, fuck! Sam!" He writhed.

Grabbing his wrists, I squeezed until he let go, afraid if I just yanked them away, my hair would come away as well. I lifted my head from him, coming off with a small pop and a grin on my face.

I rubbed his thighs with one hand while the other curled around his dick and pumped it. "Are you sure this is what you want?" I asked because I had to be sure, and if it wasn't, this would be the best stopping place for us.

"If you stop now, I won't be responsible for what happens to you later," he snapped, but his own lips were curled upwards. Without prompting and to prove his point, he used his foot to push me away and swung his legs up on the bed.

"You think you're in charge?" I chuckled softly.

Josh winked and bit his lip coyly. "One of us has to take the lead."

That was all the confirmation I required. After pushing my jeans and briefs the rest of the way off, I reached over to my nightstand and pulled it open to get the bottle of lube that hadn't been used in at least two years and the condoms that thankfully hadn't expired yet.

Climbing onto the bed, I crawled over to the side of Josh and lifted myself on my knees. I ripped the foil packet open and grabbed my lover's hand and put the condom in his hand. He got the idea and started to roll it down my hard dick, taking his sweet time. Everything about this sent me closer to the edge.

As he put the condom on me, I squeezed some of the clear lube onto my fingers and moved my hand down to his ass. He lifted his knees and spread his legs for me, needing this as much as me. Sliding my fingers between his crack, I felt for his tight hole and circled it, applying only the slightest bit of pressure so I could enjoy the way I was making him wail with pleasure.

"Fuck, Sam. Stop teasing me," he cried out.

I did always like a man who knew what he wanted in the bedroom. Pushing on his hole, my finger slid in with little resistance. I pumped it in and out a couple of times before adding a second finger, spreading them like scissors, opening him up for me.

I got a thrill at seeing him writhing on my bed, in my house, panting. His eyes were closed tightly and his head thrown back. I could see the taut muscles in his neck stand out as he whimpered and wailed. His begging increased. He arched his back and bit his lip, his hands fisting the sheets to the side of him. The sounds he made, the expression of ecstasy on his face, made me want to forget about prepping him any further and just thrust into him, but I didn't want to hurt him.

There was something sensual about prepping your lover. Watching them as they cried out, demanding that you hurry. It aroused me just as much as kissing and touching did. It was an integral part of foreplay for me.

"Jesus, Sam. I'm ready. Just fuck me already," Josh growled, and I wanted to laugh at his impatience. I never thought I'd see him this needy, but he was right. Enough. We were both ready for this. It had been years of wanting. It was time to get what we both desired.

Josh tried to get up, but I held him down with a hand on his stomach. "Face to face," I whispered, incapable of more. He nodded and lifted his legs again, holding them behind his knees with his hands.

I placed one hand beside Josh's head, and used the other one to grab my cock and leaned in to press against his hole. As much as I wanted to bury myself balls deep, I had to go slow in order not to hurt him.

Josh breathed in and out slowly. "Are you okay?" I asked. "Push against me."

He nodded and did exactly that. I knew what he was experiencing, a mixture of pleasure and pain combined.

I pushed in a little more, closing my eyes against the bliss I felt as his tight heat surrounded me. It took a little time, but I finally bottomed out and paused, waiting for him to acclimate before continuing. When he started to wiggle under me in an attempt to get closer, I bent and kissed him. The position of his legs and me over him made it hard to reach, but I wouldn't be denied.

I pulled out of him a couple of inches before sliding back in. Slow, short strokes that had him wrapping his legs around my waist and clawing my shoulders with his hands which I was positive were going to leave marks. I moved in and out of his tight hole. His leaking cock was trapped between our bodies, the friction pushing him toward the edge. I felt him begin to tighten around me, knowing that he was getting close to coming. I stopped moving, giving him a chance to move away from completion. I didn't want him coming yet. Josh's eyes met mine. Beads of sweat had formed on his forehead and his eyes were glazed over from all the stimulation.

"Why the fuck did you stop?" A whine came from his throat.

"Because you're not coming without me and I'm not done fucking you." I leaned back onto my knees, but not breaking my connection to Josh. "Jerk yourself off, I want to watch."

Josh eagerly grabbed his dick and started pumping it, slowly, teasing at first, but quickly picking up the pace when I started moving again.

Josh straddled his feet on either side of my legs and I held onto his bent knees as I started to pump into him again, my strokes longer, faster. This time, I didn't stop him when he approached the edge. Again, I felt him tighten around me right before his dick released stream after stream of white cum across his stomach.

Watching Josh come undone due to all of the pleasure I gave him, was all I needed for my own release to claim me. Falling on top of him with his cum sandwiched between us, I stretched to capture his lips in a kiss. His lips tasted salty from sweat. I licked them and then tasted his tongue. We were both out of breath and panting hard. My fingers brushed his face in amazement. Never before I had experienced something like this. At the end, it almost felt as if we'd become one, and I almost wished that were true.

His arms held me close, his legs wrapping around me. "You okay?" I questioned as I tried to roll off of him, but he kept me firmly in place—not that I minded.

Josh was out of breath when he answered, "Yeah. You?"

"Yeah." We were both educated men and we had been reduced to one syllable words.

A few more minutes passed and I tried to get up again. "I'm going to get a towel to clean us both up."

"Do you have to?" That mischievous grin was back on his face.

I chuckled. "I have to."

His legs dropped and his arms released me. I was free.

But as I got a towel and wet it with some warm water, I had to admit that I didn't want to ever be free of him. I just wondered if he felt the same way. He was about to go back to school in another state. The thoughts that had plagued me before he unceremoniously arrived on my doorstep returned.

Josh deserved more, but I didn't want him to be with anyone except me.

***

Joshua

The moment he returned with the towel, I could tell something had changed. He'd been gone two minutes and his whole countenance was different. "Sam? You all right?"

"Yeah." Shit. It was funny and cute right after sex, but right now, I needed more than a "yeah."

"Sam, look at me."

He had been wiping my stomach off and glanced up to meet my eyes. "Did I hurt you?"

I snickered. I couldn't help it. I cupped his cheek. "No, you definitely didn't hurt me," I reassured him. "I can't even begin to explain the things you made me feel. Damn."

His smile didn't quite meet his eyes. "Good."

"Talk to me, Sam. I don't know about you, but that whole thing...wow. I don't think I've ever experienced anything like it."

He flinched. "What?" I asked again.

"When are you leaving for Florida?"

I sat up and took the towel from him, throwing it off to the side somewhere. Something was very wrong. "A week, maybe more. I don't need to be back for anything for another three weeks. My job knows that I had to come home to help my mom, and the research expedition doesn't begin for about another four weeks."

"Then back to the way life was before?"

"I guess in a way it'll be."

Nodding, he got off of the bed and grabbed his underwear, sliding them on before leaving the room. I think I missed something big, but for the life of me I couldn't figure out what it was. I constantly felt like I was in the dark about things.

Getting out of bed myself, I ran after him without grabbing anything to put on. It was only the two of us in the house, what did it matter if I ran around naked? "Sam," I called after him, following him into the kitchen. "What the fuck is wrong with you?"

"Nothing. I have to get ready for class tomorrow. Today was in-service and I only had to be there a couple of hours, but school is back in session tomorrow."

I walked up to him and grabbed his arm. "We can't work on what's wrong if you don't tell me what's eating you," I groused in frustration.

He finally turned his head to meet my gaze, and what I saw there pained me. His eyes were dull and his shoulders were slumped slightly. I heard the distinct sound of him cracking his fingers. I glanced down to verify and then back up at his red face. He looked sad and pissed off at the same time. "So in a week, you'll head back and everything will go back to what it was. We won't talk for three years, you won't be back, and you'll find some other guy to fuck you whenever you're in need? Is that about right?"

"What? No, of course not."

"Then tell me how it will be."

I opened my mouth and closed it.

"And the fact that you can't, tells me everything I need to know," he spat.

My hand moved to his shoulder and in my frustration, I squeezed hard. "I don't know how it will be because I'm not a fucking psychic," I seethed. Taking in a deep breath, I forced myself to calm down before I tried again. "I don't know what is going to happen. Honestly, when I left, I never expected to see you again. I ran away to Florida and thought I'd stay there and never come back to this stupid state. My mother and I don't really get along. I mean, we can, but we tolerate each other more than anything since she hasn't exactly accepted me being gay. I think she's tried, but she's not quite there yet. And even though you're here, I never thought in a million years that you'd ever return my feelings. I figured you'd take the letter and either burn it or brush it off as some punk kid who didn't know the first thing about real emotions. So did I start seeing other guys? Yes, however, they didn't mean anything to me because I couldn't get over you. I tried and failed multiple times. So will things be the same? God, I hope not, because I'd like to think that things, at least between us, are different now."

He stepped away from me, and my heart fell into my stomach. My

74

gut clenched tightly and I started to feel lightheaded.

Leaning against the counter with his arms crossed over his chest, he gave me a hard stare. His posture convinced me that today would be both the high point and low point of my life.

I swallowed hard.

"You realize what you're saying?"

"What do you mean?" My brow furrowed in confusion.

"If you are actually saying what I think you are, you want to see if we can make a go of a relationship. You there, me here."

Hesitantly, I answered, "Yes?"

He chuckled, and that sound held the power to loosen up some of the knots in my stomach. It'd be morally wrong if he laughed right before he broke my heart. I hoped. "You don't know?" His question mocked me.

My eyes narrowed into slits as I glared at him. "I know I haven't been able to move on from you since I left. I know that today was amazing and I want more days like it. And I know I'm not ready to let you go."

His head moved up and down, and I wasn't sure what that meant. I was still slightly on guard and bewildered, but his next words eased my anxiety. "Me too." Reaching out, he grabbed my arm and jerked me toward him, wrapping his arms around me. He brushed his lips against mine gently. Not quite kissing, it was more of a mere whisper of his lips on mine. "I haven't been able to forget you or move on either."

Before I could say anything, he claimed my lips. That was the only way to explain what happened. His lips claimed me just as his body had minutes ago.

And I gladly surrendered.

Chapter 8

Joshua

After we hashed everything out, we returned to bed to enjoy ourselves, but reality eventually snuck in like a ninja and blared an alarm that had us both scrambling.

We had been happily tucked away in our own cocoon, forgetting about the rest of the world when his doorbell rang. But it didn't only ring once, someone pushed the damn thing over and over again. Practically falling over each other to get out of bed and get dressed, my head hit his nose causing him to cry out in pain. I wasn't even sure why I was getting dressed, but if he was about to have company, it'd probably be better if I wasn't lying around buck naked.

The annoying bell turned into pounding. Whomever the impatient person was had resorted to trying to get our attention two ways. The bell still chimed, but the hard thumping on the door added to our annoyance and our mild heart attacks. Assholes.

I got my pants on before Sam and ran out of the bedroom, however, when I was five feet from the door, I stopped short. The person on the other side had resorted to screaming as she pounded the door and rang the bell, and all of that was followed closely by hacking. My mother.

Sam reached me. I could feel the heat from his bare chest pressing against my back, and I almost suggested that we go back to bed and ignore my mother. We couldn't though, and at the rate she was trying to get our attention, it was only a matter of time before the cops were called.

He walked to the door, sighing heavily as he did. With one last glance over his shoulder at me, he grabbed the handle and twisted, swinging the door open before I could protest.

And there she was, leaning against the door frame, sweaty, and out of breath. She looked like death warmed over. No matter what she believed, running over here to get between Sam and I while she was sick was the wrong thing to do.

The man I loved was apparently a better humanitarian than me. As he helped my mother into the house and to the couch, I rolled my eyes and disappeared into his bedroom to grab my t-shirt, only to remember that I had left it in the living room. I didn't want to deal with her right now, so I searched through his dresser until I found another shirt. It was too big in every way except length, but it was his, and I liked the idea that it was Sam's shirt I wore. Fuck me, I was turning into a girl. Although, now that I wore something that belonged to him, the person I loved, I could see the appeal.

Loved. I did. Always had, and I knew beyond a shadow of a doubt that I always would. Maybe if I would've come out and actually said the words, he'd understand exactly why things were different now. Yes, we were still going to live in two different states—for now—but everything else had changed. We'd been dealt a different hand, and I wasn't ready to fold yet.

Lost in my own world, I didn't hear him coming into the bedroom and jumped a little when he wrapped his arms around my shoulders from behind and kissed the back of my neck. Chills of desire made me shiver as I reached up and grabbed his arms, leaning back into him. "What does she want?" I grumbled.

"To talk."

"She could have waited until I was home or until she was better."

"She could have, but you probably wouldn't have listened and would've avoided her."

I snickered. "You know me well."

"You did the same thing when you were a senior. I can remember you volunteering to rake the field after every practice so that you wouldn't have to go home. It took me a month to get it out of you."

"Things weren't rainbows and butterflies back then."

"I know they weren't, but let's at least listen to what she has to say."

Reluctantly, I nodded against his shoulder. "Fine. On one condition, though."

"What's that?" he questioned, kissing the side of my head.

"Don't listen to what she has to say. What we have is about us and us alone. Not her," I insisted as I turned around in his arms, placing my hands on his hips where his jeans met skin. I could feel the lines from the ink that resided there.

For a brief second, I thought I saw a flash of hesitancy, but it was gone before I could question it. "Deal," he agreed, and I released a breath I didn't realize I'd been holding. His lips curled up. "I brought your shirt, but I think I like you in mine. Never saw the appeal until just now."

"Me either." I winked and gave him a small kiss. I craved more, but with my mother sitting in the other room, it was probably not in our best interest.

"Go on. I'll be there in a sec." He brushed his thumb across my cheek.

Shaking my head, I refused, "No."

"Afraid?"

I noticed how the lines around his eyes became more pronounced when he smiled then. To me, it made him look sexier. I liked the small lines I could see while standing this close to him. "No, but I want to make sure you aren't going to sneak out of the window and leave me to deal with her alone," I teased. In reality, I was slightly afraid that if I went out there alone, dear old mom would get the idea to divide and conquer—not that it would work.

"We smell like sex," he stated out of the blue.

"We do." I took pride in that. Sam and I smelled of each other and sweat. It was a heady combination.

"We should probably take a shower."

"Probably."

His grin grew larger. "We don't have time though."

"Not really. Knowing my mother, she'd probably search the house for us and interrupt what could be a relaxing time."

"You're right." He sighed. Pecking my lips, he walked around me and pulled open the drawer where I'd found my current attire and grabbed a shirt for himself. On me, they looked baggy and oversized; on him, they stretched across his muscles, making it on the verge of too small. I swallowed hard and licked my lips. Damn, this man was sexy as hell…and he was mine. I trembled at the thought.

There was nothing I didn't love about him. The banter between us was lighthearted and fun, and I didn't think anyone on the planet was better looking. Plus, he was smart and cared about his students and others. He was the full package, and somehow, I lucked out and got him as my own.

Lacing his fingers with mine, he pulled me out of the room and back into the living room where my mother awaited us. Her eyes travelled to our joined hands and swept quickly upward, narrowing as she took in our faces. They then shifted to the left and widened before narrowing again. She blanched and her eyebrows pinched together. Considering how large the t-shirt I was wearing was, she probably got a small peek of the mark Sam had left on me—possibly a very large peek. I would not admit to pulling the shirt slightly to that side, but I might've.

"I see you don't listen very well, Samuel." She tried to sound regal, but she sounded out of breath and deflated. Her skin was pale and sweaty, her cheeks flushed. I wondered if she was running a fever again. Served her right for getting out of bed and coming here to threaten Sam.

"Mother," I growled in warning. At twenty-one, I was a legal adult who could make my own decisions, but apparently she didn't respect me or my choices.

"You are too young—"

"Excuse me?" I cut her off and took a step forward. Sam held me back by releasing my hand and grabbing my elbow. I stayed put, but that did not stop my mouth. "You seem to be under some delusion that I'm a child. I'm not. You also seem to believe that you can tell me who I can and can't be with. You can't. I'm twenty-one. In this country, I'm completely legal and you no longer have a say in my life."

She snorted in a very unladylike manner. "And if I cut off your funding for school?"

"Do it. You've already paid for my last semester, and if you ask for a refund, I'll find a way. There's financial aid, payment arrangements, etc. I'm almost done and you can't stop me. As a matter of fact, I also have the trust fund you and dad set up for me. I'm sure that'll take care of my last semester for school and then some."

"You can't—"

"Legally, I can." I hated arguing with her, however, this was too important to back down. Funny thing, if it were my father here in her place, I probably would have caved a little, because he'd always been there for me.

"And your Master's?"

"It's not like you were going to pay for that anyway," I reminded her. I'd heard it time and time again. I needed to get my Bachelor's degree and then a job. However, in the field I'd chosen, I needed more than just a four year degree. When I mentioned that to her, she told me I would have

79

to find a way to pay for it myself. I'd already been working on that.

Her gaze moved to Sam. "And you? Don't you care about your ruined reputation? What will the school say when they find out that you're sleeping with a student?"

"Former student."

"The thing is, that word student is still there."

"Mother!" I screamed in fury.

Her head dropped forward and her breathing became more labored. She wasn't doing well at all, and although her voice was not as strong or as loud, we still heard her when she spoke. "Fine. Do what you want, but don't come crying to me when your heart is broken." She struggled to stand from the green couch—see, favorite color—and fell backward.

Sam and I rushed forward, and when I touched her face, she was burning up. She really didn't need to be out of bed.

"Josh, call 911. Tell them we need an ambulance."

"No, no ambulance." She shook her head.

"You need a doctor," Sam insisted.

"No ambulance."

Under his breath, Sam cursed, "Fuck." He glanced up at me and said, "Grab my keys from the bowl by the door. We'll take her to the ER."

Nodding, I ran off. I was happy to be given directions to follow instead of standing there worrying about my mother. She'd pissed me off and disrespected me, but she was still my mother, and deep down, I chose to believe she did all of this out of her love for me.

Sam scooped her up and carried her to his truck, which had been unlocked when I hit the button. He laid her in the backseat and I jumped in the front passenger seat. Speeding down the freeway, we exited within a few minutes and pulled up to the ER unloading area for Mercy in Festus.

I got out of his truck and grabbed a wheelchair that sat close by, bringing it as close to the backseat as possible. Sam deposited my mother and then got back in to park while I pushed her into the cold building.

Rushing up to the window, I stammered, "My mother. She's...she's sick! She has to see a doctor, now." Memories of my father and losing him urged me on.

"Calm down," the person behind the small window stated, unconcerned. Was she a ticket agent at a movie theatre or someone who worked for a hospital? Because right now it looked like Sam had brought us to the wrong place.

"She's sick and is having a hard time breathing. She's also running a fever and was here the other day and diagnosed with the flu," I filled her in, ignoring the way she rolled her eyes.

"Please fill out this paperwork and bring—"

"What part of having a hard time breathing don't you understand?" The doors behind me opened up and I thought it was Sam. Spinning around to get his help in talking with the idiot behind the glass, I found a nurse walking in and scrolling through something on her phone. I pounced. "I need help. My mom is having a hard time breathing."

Startled, she lifted her head and then peered around me to my mother in the wheelchair. Whatever she saw spurred her into action. "Ma'am, can you hear me?" She glanced up at the person behind the window and said, "Mary, get me the oximeter." Soon, they were clipping something onto my mother's finger. "Eighty-six. Not good, but not the worst I've seen. I'll get her to the back and you can fill out the paperwork," she told me.

It gave me a small level of relief knowing that my mother was being taken care of, however, I didn't know the answers to most of the questions on the forms. I'd just sat down to attempt answering them when Sam came in and sat next to me. Together we pored over the forms, but he knew less than I did.

Returning the clipboard to the woman behind the glass, I said, "I did as much as I could. My mom will have to give you the rest of the info."

"Thank you. Would you like to go back?"

I lifted one of my eyebrows in question. Suddenly the nurse stepped in and this person can be nice to me? In my head, I called her a bitch, but to her face, I smiled. "Yes, please."

"She's in room 11."

Walking over to Sam, I said, "We can go back. Want to come with me?" I desperately needed him to say yes, but was afraid he'd say no.

"Let's go." He stood up and wrapped his arm around my waist.

My shoulders slumped in relief, and I sagged against him. He wasn't abandoning me. I wasn't quite sure why I thought he would, but after everything that had happened today, and now my mother on top of that, I feared the worst deep within me.

It was still the flu. They loaded her up with fluids, gave her some meds, and sent her on her way after a breathing treatment brought her oxygen stats back up. I knew it was wrong to think it, but I wouldn't be surprised if she had done all of this on purpose.

Dropping her off at her house, I helped her get settled and then turned around to leave. "You're not staying?" she called after me.

I halted, but did not face her. "No. I'm going back over to Sam's and getting your car. We'll drop it off and then go back to his place."

"What if I get bad again?"

"911?" I was a first rate asshole.

"Joshy—"

"Mom, I love you, I do, but I'm not the little boy you used to take to the park and play with. I grew up. Somewhere during the time you started to work more and spend less time at home, I grew up, discovered who I am, and became a man. I'd like to think I'm a good one. I make good grades, work hard, and will graduate at the end of fall. Whom I choose to love shouldn't matter to you. The only thing that should matter is that I'm happy, and Sam does that for me. I loved him before dad died, and after, he was the only thing that kept me afloat when I wanted to drown. You didn't see that. You couldn't see that." I slowly spun around to face her, my heart pounding in my chest, and my eyes burning with unshed tears. "I didn't blame you for that then, and I don't now because you were grieving the loss of the love of your life. But answer me this, can you honestly tell me that you would've rather had the time you had together, or would it have been better if you'd never met him?"

She sucked in a shaky breath, her lip trembling. "I don't want to see you hurt."

"Which is better? They say it is better to have loved and lost than never to have loved at all."

Her finger swept through the air in an arc. "The first one."

"If he hurts me, I'll lick my wounds and then move on, but I have this chance, something I've wanted for years, and I have to go for it. If I don't, I'll regret it for the rest of my life."

"A nice catholic girl—"

"Would never satisfy me or make me happy. Besides, in this day and age, gay marriage is legal and if I wanted kids, I could always adopt or go through a surrogate." I gave her a small smile, praying she would finally accept me as I was.

Her eyes moved to the window. I wondered what she saw. Did she see the view, or something else? It was the same window that my father had installed and made sure it was perfect after we broke it. She stared through it a lot, something I noticed after my father had passed away.

"Call home more often, and if you need me..." She didn't finish, she didn't need to.

"I know. I will, but I'm not leaving for Florida yet. I mean, Sam and I will go and get your car and we'll be right back."

"But you're not staying."

"We'll stay." Guilt crashed over me and I gave in, however, I had stipulations. "As in both of us. No more threatening him or trying to run him off."

She didn't smile, but she sat up a little straighter. And I felt even guiltier for my previous attitude. "Do you want something to eat?" I asked. "It's late and you haven't eaten." We had been at the hospital for hours, leaving after it was nearing eleven at night. I hoped Sam didn't kill me for volunteering to stay.

Shaking her head, she said, "No. I'm just really tired."

"Then how about we get you to bed. You can sleep. When Sam and I get back, we'll go down to the basement."

She couldn't seem to lift herself off of the couch. I knew the flu had taken a lot out of her, but it bothered me that it had made her so weak. Maybe it was nothing more than old memories of a bad time that fed my anxiety and concern, but that argument didn't make me feel better.

I grabbed her arm and wrapped it around my shoulders, holding her wrist with my right hand. I wrapped my other arm around her waist and lifted. She weighed next to nothing, and again I was struck by how slight she'd become.

Getting her into bed was easy because I was able to swing her up in my arms and lift her. Something I hadn't been able to do three years ago. Covering her with a blanket, I noticed she'd already fallen asleep. She still sounded a little raspy, and I needed to pick up her prescriptions, but compared to the way she looked earlier, I'd take this version. "Feel better, Mom," I whispered as I leaned down to kiss her forehead. I'd never seen her so sick, and I desperately prayed that she'd get better.

Quietly, I closed her bedroom door and then had to stifle a scream when I saw Sam leaning against the wall near the short hallway. "Don't do that," I chastised, and at the same time, I told my heart to calm down.

"Everything okay?" he asked as he pushed himself away from the wall, opening his arms for me to come to him.

I walked into those strong arms and let him hold me, to share a little of his strength with me. "She's sleeping."

"How are you holding up?"

"She's sick and I can't ever remember seeing her like this."

"You're scared."

"Yeah."

"She's not going to leave you like your dad."

"I know."

He sighed and squeezed me a little tighter. "Are you hungry?"

Even though I had mentioned food to my mother, I hadn't actually felt hungry until Sam said something. As if on cue, my stomach shouted with a distinctive gurgle. "I guess I could eat." I chuckled.

"Let's go grab some food, since I'm sure neither of us feels like cooking. After that we'll swing by Walgreens and get your mother's medicine."

"And then?"

He somehow understood my question. "And then we'll stop and get some clothes for me and come back here."

Lifting my head where it had been resting on his shoulder and against his neck, I kissed him. "Thank you."

"Come on before I change my mind." Although he sounded impatient and harsh, the smile on his face, which made his eyes crinkle at the corners, told me otherwise.

"All right." I stepped back and grabbed his hand to pull him toward the door. The sooner we left, the sooner I got food, and the sooner we were in my bedroom together. I couldn't bring myself to have sex with him under my mother's roof, and I had a feeling Sam felt the same way, but cuddling could be just as intimate. I loved the feel of his large muscles curling around me, molding his body to mine.

***

Samuel

If I had my druthers about it, I would've stayed at my house, but I didn't want to leave Josh alone. When he walked out of his mother's room, he appeared worn out and tired, almost defeated with his hunched shoulders and droopy head. I had enough insecurities about us, I needed him to be the confident one until I could catch up. And admittedly, the longer I sat out in the car waiting for him to come back, the more the panic began to grow.

Earlier today, he'd projected himself as a confident young man who refused to accept his mother's prejudice against our relationship. Hell, for that matter, he wouldn't take "no" from me either. Josh was headstrong and over the top. One of the many things that had captured me and held on, nagging me daily until I realized how I actually felt about him. I loved him. I still had doubts to work through, and I wasn't completely convinced that I was the right man for him, but I owed it to both of us to try...at least until he returned to Tallahassee. Once he left, everything would be different, and I wasn't sure we could survive it.

I also wasn't completely convinced it was all worth it. He was younger, good looking, smart, and had a great personality...not to mention he had other men throwing themselves at him in college. I feared one day, he would realize this was nothing more than a lingering crush. I was scared that now he had me, he'd leave me. Not right away, but eventually.

Unless I left first.

Shaking my head, ridding myself of that pessimistic thought, I grabbed his hand, lacing my fingers with his as we drove off. My brother needed to get out of my head. He was the reason I was questioning everything. I wasn't even sure how or when it happened; I'd never let him or his views on gay relationships get to me before.

"You okay?" This time it was Josh who asked me.

One side of my lip lifted in a half grin. "Yeah. Been a long day."

"I know. If you don't feel comfortable or don't want to stay with me tonight, I'll understand."

I believed him, but I could also hear the tremor in his voice. He'd understand, but he also would rather I stayed. For him, I would. "No, I'm just tired. I'll come back with you." The thing was, as much as he coveted my company, I did the same with him. I wished I could be selfish and keep him all to myself until the last possible second when he had to return to Florida. And even then, I had the urge to hold onto him for dear life

85

and never let him go.

Another first. My brother had never gotten inside my head, and I'd never wanted someone so desperately that I'd become a selfish man. The power of Josh.

I peered at him and noticed him watching me with a slightly goofy grin on his face. Seeing it, made me chuckle. "What?"

He shook his head slightly, but that smile never left his handsome face. "Nothing."

Lifting a brow in question, my eyes returned to the road. "Nothing?"

"It's just…" His hand squeezed mine, and he may as well have squeezed my heart. "When I first saw you, it was a week before school. I only caught a glimpse of you before you disappeared. I almost thought I imagined you."

"A week, but I thought it was the first day of school."

"I was up at the school for student council and to help with freshman orientation."

"I don't remember you being on student council."

"I wasn't, but I was the sophomore class secretary and the class officers from all of the grades were asked to help with orientation."

That I did remember. Throughout his time in high school, he'd been a class officer, not that they did much in our school. Helped out here and there, passed on information occasionally, and helped plan prom, but that was about the extent of their duties.

"I honestly thought that I had made you up because the night before I was talking with one of my girlfriends about guys we liked. She'd just started dating the JV quarterback, Todd Banes, and I asked what she saw in him. It got us on a tangent and we described our ideal guy. That night, I had this weird dream where I saw my perfect guy, and then the next day, I caught that brief glimpse of you. I honestly thought my mind was playing tricks on me. Then on the first day of school, there you were talking to Mrs. Lopez, our resident torturer."

"She did not torture you. She taught you Spanish." I chuckled.

"You didn't take her class."

"You're right, and from what I've heard, I don't want to."

"Lucky asshole," he muttered under his breath and we both laughed some more. It felt good to relax and let loose with him.

"So anyway, I saw you standing there talking to her, and I was gaping

86

at you from the senior lockers. I came around the corner and basically screeched to a halt when I saw you. And then our star varsity linebacker, Eric Marin, was in a rush and ran smack into me, throwing me into the lockers. I had a purple line on my arm from where it hit the corner of the lockers for a week. Poor guy felt guilty and tried to apologize before he ran down the hall and toward the gym. You stopped him for running in the halls as he passed you."

"Does this mean it was the concussion that made you think you were in love with me?" I teased him. Somehow, knowing this history alleviated some of the anxiety I felt.

"It might have knocked a few screws loose—that man was built like a brick wall, which is probably why his nickname in school was the Brick Wall—but about the only thing it did teach me was not to gape at a teacher in the middle of a crowded hallway with football players around. I had to be more careful when I…let's say, observed you." He snickered.

After we drove through White Castle for food and grabbed his mother's meds, I noticed he had become very quiet and somber. "Josh?"

"When my dad died, I pushed everyone away. I didn't want to deal with life. I even thought about ending it. He'd been my best friend, and the first person I told that I was gay. He even broke the news to my mother for me. That night, there was a lot of yelling in the house. He was there for me, guided me, punished me when I needed it, and encouraged me in everything. When I told him about you, he only told me to wait until graduation before I confessed. He never tried to change my mind or tell me I was an idiot for thinking my feelings were real. The last memory I have of being really close to my mother, I was six and she took me to the park when my dad had to work overtime. Back then, their roles were reversed. My dad was the main breadwinner and my mom was finishing up her Master's degree while she was a stay at home mom. After she graduated and found a job, within a month, my dad got notice that he was getting laid off. I can't remember how long it took him to find a job, but he eventually found one and hated it. He said he realized what was important when he had been the one staying home with me. My mom started to work longer hours and began moving up the corporate ladder. Dad quit his job as soon as he found a new one, and that's where he stayed until he passed away."

"I didn't know."

His head dipped in a small nod. "I think I was in first or second grade. After that, whenever I got sick, he was the one who stayed home.

If the school needed to talk to a parent, my dad showed up. He was there for everything. There were times my mom didn't get home until midnight. On average, I didn't see her until I was about to head to bed. This is going to sound bad, but in some ways, it was like being raised in a single parent home. I think she was afraid of something happening again and she didn't want to worry about money. Eventually, I think it consumed her. The thing is, she made enough that half of every one of Dad's checks were put in a trust fund for me. I know she loved us, and I think sometimes she did want to be there, but it wasn't in the cards." His voice cracked and I squeezed his hand, the hand that had only left my grip for the time it took to get food and the medicine.

Pulling into my driveway, we sat there. I could tell he had more to get off his chest.

Clearing his throat, he continued, "When my dad died, my world imploded and I couldn't…I didn't know…" He drew in a shaky breath. "I didn't know how to cope. I'd never felt grief like that before. It consumed me. The world used to be full of color and then it wasn't. Going to a baseball game without my dad…It just wasn't the same. I hit bottom and I thought about things I should have never thought about. One of the reasons I didn't, was you. I no longer cared about baseball or school, but there was still you." His voice warbled.

My chest felt tight and tears blurred my vision as I listened to his confession.

"I could hear you in my ear, see you in my head telling me to pull my head out of my butt and run the bases. And then when you came looking for me, I somehow knew everything was going to be okay." He turned his head and met my eyes, his own tears falling down his cheeks. I used my free hand to brush them away. "You aren't replacing my dad, but you did save me. I loved you then and it's never changed."

I had no words. I didn't know what to say or how to respond to any of that. I didn't try. Leaning toward him, I pressed my lips to his in a slow, sweet kiss.

My brother could go to hell. Josh was mine.

Chapter 9

Samuel

The night Josh spilled his guts, we might have gone inside and made love once more before we showered and I packed a bag to take with us— very much did that. And his words made me realize something, nothing is guaranteed. It would be difficult to manage and it may not work out in the end, but this was our time to see where this led, our moment to shine and to see if we really had something between us.

Fear would sabotage us. Indecision could end us. But even if we were afraid, jumping in with both feet might save us.

We'd been staying at his house for the past week, and I had to say, it was more than a little awkward. I would run my hand through his hair, touch him innocently, or give him a kiss, and I could practically feel her eyes on me, judging me. I expected some of it, but this much was nerve wrecking. She didn't say anything, though, and seemed to accept us. Maybe. Luckily, she was on the mend. However, that also meant Josh's time here was coming to an end, and I hoped it would only be temporary.

During the day, I went to school; and after baseball practice, which Josh had started to show up to on a daily basis, we would either go to my house for some alone time away from the prying eyes of his mother, or we would go out to eat. It was our time and we had to get as much of it as possible.

A week had passed since the day he miraculously showed up on my doorstep, and in that time, I hadn't thought about my brother at all. Josh made me happier than I'd been in a long time. Even people at work were noticing. Finding someone who loved you had a way of changing a lot of things.

Today, though, Josh hadn't been able to come to practice and help me put the team through drills. Instead, we had plans to meet up at my house by five. When I got there, I didn't see his car and figured he hadn't made it yet. I'd been wrong. So wrong.

Sticking my key into the lock, it opened before I could turn it. My eyes darted up and I could already feel the fury building in my gut, burning a hole in my sanity. "What the hell are you doing here, Charles? And how the fuck did you get in my house?" I demanded, seething. I almost wished I had a gun so I could shoot my brother and tell the cops he was trespassing after breaking in. Too bad I didn't have one handy.

"Is that any way to talk to your brother?" He sniffed, looking down his nose at me. The hair on top of his head was almost all gone, and he would have been better off shaving off what little he had left. Instead, he tried a comb over, which didn't work well with his dark brown hair that had just enough wave in it to prevent it from completely combing over his pale head.

He was taller than me by a couple of inches, slender, resembling a twig more than a man. His suit hung on him as if he bought it off the rack instead of had it made for him, but I knew better. He bought them that way because for some reason he believed it added bulk. It didn't. It made him look like he borrowed the suit from Andre the Giant instead of a tailor.

I used my shoulder and pushed him out of the way. "Last I checked, you were my only brother, but that doesn't automatically make you my favorite. In fact, I'm pretty sure I told you to leave me alone and forget I existed. Care to tell me why you're breaking and entering before I call the cops?"

"I'm not. I had a key." He sniffed again.

Spinning around quickly, I pegged him with a withering glare, watching him take a step back, practically shrinking in on himself. He may be taller and older, but I had the muscle to physically throw him out of my house. The only reason I didn't was because I wanted to know how the hell he had gotten into my house with the key. There were two people with keys to this house. Me and Josh…shit! "Where did you get a fucking key?"

"Your boy toy came over and nicely handed it over when I explained who I was."

"What did you say to Josh?" The expression seeing red had nothing on me right now. I was pissed and seeing black. I felt only rage, cared only about pounding my brother into the ground. The fact that he was cowering meant nothing to me. "Charles, what did you say to Josh?" I seethed, repeating myself because he never answered the first time.

"I told him that you didn't have time for him any longer and that he needed to leave before I reported him to the police for entrapment," he stammered breathlessly. He'd closed the door, but hadn't moved from his spot near it. His body shook as his eyes darted around, and there was a distinct tremor in his voice.

Good. He should be afraid, because gone was the mild mannered teacher. I was feeling violent. When he saw me pull back my arm, he covered his face. I punched him in the gut, making him double over and drop to the ground.

"How dare you!" I yelled. Charles was a pathetic excuse for a man. As soon as he dropped, he curled into a ball to protect himself.

"I dare because…" His face was red and becoming mottled. He sounded like he was having a hard time breathing, and I didn't care.

When he lifted his head, I grabbed him by the throat and forced him to stand. His feet scrambled after him and his legs lifted his body, knowing if they didn't, it would make things a lot more painful than they currently were. His fingers tried and failed to pry my hand away from his neck.

I ignored him and demanded, "What happened to Josh?" Charles's reasons for being here were no longer my main concern, I only cared about Josh.

Drool ran down his chin and neck, his face became redder, and his eyes were bulging a little. "He ran away like a scared little boy. What, now you're going for jailbait? He isn't leg—" He whispered, spit flying out of his mouth. He struggled to talk before I forced him to shut up.

I squeezed my hand, cutting off his oxygen and his words. Letting up on the tight hold, I made sure my grip was still firm. "Just so you know, that 'boy' you're making fun of is my boyfriend and more of a man than you will ever be. Not only that, but he's perfectly legal and twenty-one, about to graduate with his degree in Marine Biology, and he did it on his own, which is more than I can say for you. You had to have our father make a way for you, and you continue to ride on his coattails. If you've hurt Josh, I'll kill you. I know where to hide bodies so that they will never be found. Biology can tell us a lot about our surroundings."

He swallowed hard. I could feel his Adam's apple bobbing under my palm. "If you were so special to him, why did he run away? Why didn't he defend himself?" He snapped, grasping at straws.

"Threatening someone with legal action has a way of making them hightail it out of here, but don't believe for one second that this changes things between him and me. We're still together, and we will continue to be well into the future."

"You should be with a wo—"

I squeezed again. "No, I shouldn't be. I should be with Josh, and as soon as I kick you out, that's where I'll be."

When I let him breathe again, he sucked in buckets of air. "You need to come home and marry the girl Father picked out." He rushed, his eyes tearing from being choked.

"No, I don't."

"He's dying!" Charles screamed.

"And that is my problem because…why exactly?" It sounded callous and uncaring, but it was true. My father all but disowned me when he found out I was gay, and even before that, our relationship was strained and awkward. At one point, I tried to make Marcus Cayden happy, but I quickly realized that I never would. Ergo, unlike Charles, I didn't kiss my father's ass or try to follow in his footsteps. I had my own destiny to fulfill, and it was for me to decide what that was. No one else would ever tell me who I was supposed to be.

"Because he said if you come back, he's willing to forgive everything."

"Forgive? What the hell is there to forgive? I don't need Father's forgiveness. So…no, thank you."

"He also said that he would leave you half of the estate and make you the CEO."

A dark, bitter laugh welled up from deep within me. "I'm surprised you're here, Charles. I thought you were gunning for that position."

"I'm under strict orders to bring you back." And there was the crux of it. My brother was my father's trusty lap dog, even if it meant Charles got the short end of the stick.

My father and my brother could kiss my tattooed ass. "That's not happening. Why don't you go back and tell him I died and couldn't reach me in the beyond."

"Samuel, I can't do that and you know it."

"I know a lot of things. You can, but you are too afraid of what he'll do to you. I'm not going back."

"Samuel," he whined. It amazed me sometimes that he was a year older than me.

"You need to leave."

"I'm not leaving until you come back."

92

I reached into my pocket and simultaneously grabbed my phone while swiping my thumb across the screen to unlock it. Holding it up to my ear, I spoke, "Can you please send an officer? I have someone who's broken into my house and is still on the premises." His eyes widened in fear as all color drained from his face. "Yes, the address is—"

"I'm leaving, but we aren't done with this conversation," Charles announced, breaking free from my loosened grip and opening the door. He stormed out of my house acting like the hounds of hell were nipping at his heels.

"I think we are," I mumbled, pocketing my phone again. My brother was a scared idiot, which played in my favor this time since he believed I somehow managed to swipe and call 911 at the same time. I had no doubt that he would be back. He wasn't done with this...whatever the hell it was. When my father sent him on a mission, Charles hated to fail. I needed to be on guard.

Before that though, Josh was my priority. I had no idea what he thought after being run off by my brother. Damage control wasn't exactly my strong suit either. Then again, I'd never had to clean up something of this magnitude. If it didn't work out in the past, then it didn't work out. I was forever cleaning up after my brother. But this time, it mattered. This time, I needed to fix everything.

A soft knock at my door made me want to rip the blasted thing off its hinges and rip the perpetrator a new asshole, especially since I somehow knew it was Charles. "I thought—" I swallowed anything else I was going to say and was struck dumb. It wasn't my brother or a neighbor checking to see what the ruckus was about, it was Josh. His cheeks were pink, his face blotchy, and his eyes were wet. If Charles made him cry, I'd kill him.

"You thought?" he asked, his shoulders slumped.

"I was just about to call you."

"I parked down the street when I left and waited for that guy to leave."

I held the door open a little wider. "Come on in. I think we need to talk."

His shoulders lifted and fell as he hefted a loud sigh. "Later? I just want you to tell me he's full of shit and take me to bed."

A small grin graced my face. I grabbed his arm and pulled him against my chest, slamming the door once he was inside. "Completely full of shit, and I've told him to pretend I don't exist, but he won't listen to me."

His hand snaked its way into my sweatpants and wrapped around my dick. "I haven't showered yet," I told him. My tongue darted out to lick my lips.

"Shower later. You're just going to get sweaty again," he whispered against my mouth, his breath warm and smelling like peppermint.

The invitation was too much to ignore any longer. Jerking his hand out of my pants, I held onto his wrist and pulled him into my bedroom as quickly as possible. One of these days, I might have to stash the essentials in other places around the house, but for now, they were only in my room and I had to fuck him, to assure myself that he was still here, still mine, and that we had made it past this small hurdle together.

Bursting into my room, I spun around and grabbed his face to kiss him, hard and demanding. He matched me kiss for kiss, our tongues melding together until they felt like they were fused to each other.

I moved one of my hands down his face, his neck, and his body. Moving lower and lower, dropping to his ass and squeezing for a moment, before it descended even further. I gripped his thigh, squeezing and putting pressure on it so that he would lift it. Josh took the hint and wrapped his leg around my hip, digging his heel into the globe of my butt. His lips broke from mine when I ground my hardness into his, our breathing erratic.

"Too many clothes." I swallowed hard, willing everything to slow down. I wanted to make love to him, to savor our connection, but the way we were moving, we'd be done before we really began.

Taking a giant step away from him, I lifted my shirt and fought to get it off, ripping it at the collar. I didn't care, and grinned when he appeared to be struggling with his jeans. We were a mess, but this was who we were. Imperfectly perfect for each other.

When we were both naked, he pushed me toward the bed. "Lie on your back," he ordered. Up to this point, I'd been the one to take charge sexually. Seeing him like this was erotic, and if he wanted to do the fucking tonight, I'd probably let him.

Clambering onto the bed, I rested my head on a pillow and waited with my eyes closed, looking forward to whatever he had planned. The sound of the nightstand drawer opening and closing told me he was getting everything ready. My dick twitched in anticipation. And the next thing I felt was a moist heat swirling around the head of my dick, and then licking my slit.

"Fuuuuck!" I shouted. His tongue drove me crazy when it was in my mouth, but this sent me to another galaxy. He placed a hand on my hip and pressed down, while the other one wrapped around my length and pumped. His mouth engulfed me, taking me in a few inches. It felt amazing.

"No, I can't." I grabbed his hair and pulled, my hands fisting in his waves. "I can't hold it. Can't wait. I'm too close."

"Then come." A hint of amusement laced his words. His eyes squinted up at me and one corner of his mouth curled up.

"No."

"Yes. I'll tie you up if you don't listen."

I quit breathing.

***

Joshua

I'd only been teasing about tying him up, but when he sucked in his breath and closed his eyes like he had experienced the greatest pleasure known to man, I considered following through with my threat. He pulled my hair, almost painfully so, when I returned my focus to his cock, but I pinched his thigh and he finally relaxed his grip a little. It was my turn to have my way with him. This was the first time I'd had the chance to give him a blow job, and I wasn't going to let him cut me off or rush me. This was about his pleasure as well as mine.

His dick was wider than mine, but mine was a little longer, and I became curious to know what it would feel like to slide my dick into his ass, his heat surrounding me. Not today though. After what happened with his brother, I wanted to feel him pounding into me.

I sat parked at the end of the block, watching and waiting for Sam to get home. When he did, I tried to call out a warning to him, but a delivery truck had chosen then to pull up across the street and drowned out my yell. His brother's threats infuriated me, but it was so much more. I was also confused because I didn't understand why this person would say

95

these things to me, and for a split second, I questioned if this stranger really spoke on behalf of my lover. And then shame for that brief moment of weakness when I thought Sam might agree with him. On top of everything though, what Sam's brother did hurt.

I lost my chance to warn Sam when his door swung open, so I bided my time, believing Sam would throw that jerk out. I counted the minutes, my gut churning the longer I sat there without a clue about what was happening in the house.

And then Sam's brother left. Running away like a scared rabbit, tripping over his own feet, and landing flat on his face in the dirt.

His hand found its way into my hair again and pulled. "Hey, you okay?" Sam asked when I lifted my head. He'd known my mind had wandered, and I wasn't sure how.

Forcing a smile, I nodded and attempted to dip my head again, but he stopped me. "Talk to me." He sat up and pulled me onto his lap, holding me tightly. "What's wrong?"

I straddled his hips, momentarily forgetting about our nakedness. My eyes met his concerned gaze. His brow was furrowed and he rubbed his thumb across my cheek. "Your brother's an asshole."

"Yeah, he is. You're being kind. I think I've called him a bastard, fucktard, shithead, and a few more choice words. You're lucky it was only him. My father's even worse." He tried to laugh, but it came out sounding like a strangled cat.

He lifted his other hand, cupping my face with both. "I'm sorry. You shouldn't have had to deal with him at all. Do me a favor and don't listen to anything he has to say."

"I didn't. I don't believe him, it's just…hearing him say all that stuff, and then everything with my mom, I wondered if maybe you were having second thoughts about us."

"No, never."

A grin tugged at my lips. "You were the person who told me 'never say never.'"

"I did, but this one time, I mean it. I love you, Josh. I'm not having second thoughts about anything. Maybe in the beginning, but today I realized I've never been surer about anything in my life." He looked so earnest and serious.

My heart skidded to a halt. "You…you love me?" I stammered, unsure I heard him correctly.

His smile was genuine, his eyes crinkling. "Yeah, I love you."

"I love you too." I couldn't manage anything more than a whisper before I closed my eyes, leaned forward, and locked our lips together. Feeling his tongue tracing my lips, I opened my mouth and welcomed the invasion.

Our frenzied pace from earlier disappeared. We took our time, savoring this moment. Every touch, every kiss, reinforced our feelings for each other. And when he rolled us over and gently slid his cock into me, he moved slowly, taking his time.

During the past week, we'd come here to escape so that we could be intimate and have some alone time. Those times were more about satisfaction and finishing quickly since we had to be back at my mother's house. This time it was different. We moved slowly, reverently, without worry or concern about anyone else. It was about us.

His strokes were long and slow, and the hand that he wrapped around my cock moved in time with his hips. I was in sensory overload, careening to completion. My nails scratched the bedsheets, my hands fisted the material and twisted it. My mouth opened in a silent yell as he hit the perfect spot inside me.

He was a master and I was his puppet.

"Sam," I whimpered. I was close, so close.

His grip on my dick squeezed a little harder, almost painfully. I was spiraling out of control. A drop of sweat landed on my chest. We were both covered in a fine sheen, but seeing that, feeling it land, made me happy. For whatever reason, it gave me a small sense of peace right before I arched my back and ejaculated all over my stomach.

Sam continued to pump within me. Once. Twice. And then he groaned, his hips jerked, and he became still. A minute later, he rolled to the side of me, out of breath, throwing his arm over his eyes.

That experience surpassed anything I'd ever experienced before with him or anyone else. Then again, no one could measure up to Sam. My imagination included.

"Would it be horrible if I suggested we stay here tonight? I really don't want to have to go spend time with your mother right now. I'd rather spend tonight with you and only you," he stated.

I couldn't disagree at all. "No. Want to shower, and then you can order a pizza while I call her?" I didn't want to go home either. This bed called to me, and I'd much rather stay here with this man...my man.

97

"Pizza?"

"They deliver and then we don't have to think about going out."

"Do you still like extra pepperoni?"

"Imo's?" I made a face and he snorted with mirth.

"Cecil Whittaker's."

"Then yes, but don't let your pineapple come anywhere near my pepperoni." I wasn't sure what it was about Imo's pizza, but I didn't particularly care for it, which made me an oddball in this area. Most people from St. Louis raved about it. The only thing I liked from that restaurant was its toasted ravioli. Cecil Whittaker's on the other hand, I loved.

Laughing, he glanced down at my crotch. "I think it's too late for that."

"So wrong." I guffawed.

After we settled down from our laughing fit, he suggested, "Come on. Let's get cleaned up and then I'll put in our order." Neither of us moved an inch.

"We're pathetic." I snickered.

"You wrung me out."

"I could say the same thing about you." My hand patted the bed between us, searching for his hand and grasping hold when I found it. "I wouldn't have it any other way." I turned my head and glanced at him. He was smiling.

"Me either." He leaned over and pressed his lips to mine. When he was done, he spoke softly, "Come on. Let's wash up before you get things started and we forget to call your mom."

"That right there is a mood killer."

He threw his head back and laughed louder, rolling off of the bed on his side. "I promise to get you back in the mood after you call her. If we don't, she'll probably come over with a gun next time."

I rolled my eyes at his horrible joke, but shook my head as I snickered a little more. My mother may not completely accept our relationship, but she was working on it. At least she let Sam stay with me and left us alone for the most part. However, she informed us this past week that she'd started taking shooting lessons at Top Gun, the gun range down the road from our house.

Coming around to my side of the bed, he stared down at me in all his naked glory. We hadn't bothered with the lights, too wrapped up in each other when we came in here and we still had plenty of daylight left, but sometime while we were utterly wrapped up in ourselves, the moonlight and streetlights had claimed the night and their light snaked through the open curtains. It gave me just enough light to see him, and I didn't think I'd ever get sick of looking at him. For someone who was thirty-five, he looked better than most college kids I knew.

"Come on, Sleeping Beauty," he teased, poking me in the ribs.

"I'm coming." I didn't move a muscle, simply stared at the man beside me. The very man who had confessed his feelings for me. I never thought I'd hear him say that he loved me. If I was dreaming, I never wanted to wake up.

"I could carry you, but what about your man card?" Again he mocked, covering his mouth and gasping.

Not funny, and yet, I snorted and bit my lip to suppress my own laughter. Once I thought it was somewhat under control, I asked, "How would anyone know if we're the only ones who see it?" I lifted an eyebrow, silently challenging him.

His smile made my heart thunder and my pulse quicken. It sounded stupid and cheesy, and I was all right with that.

He leaned over me. Kissing my neck, he moved upwards and bit my jaw before locking his lips with mine. I could kiss him forever and die a happy man. More cheesiness, but I didn't care.

Wrapping my arms around his neck, I held him in place and took from him just as much as I received. And when he pulled back, Sam couldn't go far since I held him prisoner. He laughed, and my heart skipped. "Shower?" he asked softly.

The feel of my cum drying on my stomach demanded I get in the shower, however, the feel of his body over mine trumped all else.

He laughed again and shoved his hands behind my back, his nails slightly scraping me as he lifted me into a sitting position. Then he moved his hands to my legs, wrapping them around his waist. Grabbing my ass, he stood up straight with me in his arms and walked straight into the en suite bathroom.

It was a large room, almost the size of the "office" at home. It had a large shower with three showerheads, a claw-footed tub, and double sinks. The counters were neutral tan, but the walls were a sky blue. It reminded me of a cloudless day in Florida.

He dropped me on the cold counter and I scrambled off, almost falling face first on the tiled floor, but I managed to catch myself.

I heard him chuckling with his back to me as he turned on the water. This time I knew he was laughing at me instead of with me. And that was all right. I was sure my sudden jump was a comical sight to behold.

"When do you think you're going back?" His question caught me unaware.

"I don't know," I said softly. His back was to me and I could only see him nod once. Honestly, I hadn't thought about heading back home. I'd been enjoying our time together too much and didn't want to leave him, but it was time to act like the adult I claimed I was. I still had to graduate and if I didn't show up, that wouldn't happen.

Silence filled the room except for the spraying water. Dread filled my stomach, and I suddenly feared the magic between us might disappear the moment I headed south. "Sam?"

He cleared his throat. "Shower's ready."

"Sam."

Slowly, he turned around to face me, his hand reaching out to me. "We'll make it work."

I stepped up to him without saying anything.

"Let's go back to three minutes ago. Pretend the last couple of minutes didn't happen. It's just that I like having you here and I'm going to miss you," he muttered as he pushed me into the shower.

"You're not the only one. I'll miss you too. I finally got what I wanted and now I have to leave."

"We'll figure it out." He lifted a hand and I thought he was going to do some sweet, romantic gesture. Wrong. Unexpectedly, he pushed my head under the spray, causing me to sputter. But then I felt his hands in my hair, massaging my head as he washed it for me. A simple act that was also so sensual.

After he washed my hair, he grabbed a washcloth and moved it across my body. He didn't leave one inch of me untouched.

And when he was done, it was my turn. I'd had this fantasy about kissing each one of his tattoos, and I'd yet to fulfill it. Tonight, I planned on making it happen. Washing his hair, I started to move my lips over his shoulder, tracing the outlines of one of his tats with my tongue…until I got shampoo in my mouth and had to spit multiple times. Movies and books made it look and sound so easy. Note to Hollywood, when washing your boyfriend's hair, soap could run down the neck and shoulders—not could, always.

I hadn't had my mouth washed out with soap since I exclaimed, "Fucking hell," after destroying one of Mrs. Byrd's prized tulip plants in the third grade. My mother heard me and wanted to teach me a lesson, although she seemed more concerned about my language than the plant.

"You all right there, Josh?" Sam checked on me, but it came out in a stammer since he was chuckling when he spoke.

"Yeah, but I feel like I'm eight again and getting my mouth washed out with soap for cussing." I lifted my face to the showerhead above us and opened my mouth. Swishing with the water, I spit it out.

"I can attest, you are all adult." His hand rubbed my back.

This man had come a long way. Only a week ago, he tried to hold himself back around me.

We'd both come a long way.

Grinning, I stepped up to him again and moved the sponge across his chest, moving it down his stomach. "We'd have a big problem if that were the case."

"Only big?" He lifted one of his brows.

"Huge."

We broke apart again, howling with laughter. After that, our shower consisted of a lot of touching, kissing, and amusement. This was us, and I wouldn't have it any other way. If we took ourselves too seriously, I was afraid of what would happen. There were things that some might consider doomed our relationship, but we had much more than that between us. We could make it if we kept in mind the positive more than the negative. This was our relationship, and what others thought, did not matter.

Watching him get out of the shower, the way his butt flexed and swayed slightly, I almost neglected my mother and pulled him back to bed. In fact, I was reaching for his arm when he peered over his shoulder. "Call first, dessert later."

I rolled my eyes. "Fine, but dessert better be good."

"I promise it will be very filling." I wasn't sure how he was able to keep a straight face, with nothing more than a cocky smirk on his face when he said that.

I stood there dumbly, my mouth hanging open and frozen in my tracks as he left the room. How was I supposed to call my mother when

101

he said stuff like that? The moment the words left his mouth, my dick sprang to life.

"Your mom's on the phone," I heard from the other room.

I hadn't moved an inch and hadn't heard the phone ring. I still stood in the shower, water dripping off of my body. Only Sam could do this to me.

Moving more like a zombie than a person, I grabbed a towel from the rack and stumbled into the bedroom. He handed me the phone, and all I could mutter was, "Uh, thanks." He was laughing at me when he left me alone in the room. One of these days, I'd get him back. It'd probably take multiple attempts, but I had an inkling that I'd relish every moment of every day.

Whoa. The future. I was grinning like a fool thinking about us together years from now.

"Joshua?" The sound of my mother's voice snapped me out of my reverie.

Shaking my head, I put the phone up to my ear as I wrapped the towel around my waist. "Sorry about that. Hey."

"Hey? That's all you got to say. Do you know what time it is?"

I almost snapped, "No, I was too busy having heart stopping, bone weary sex with my boyfriend. And I'm not a child anymore," but I refrained. My eyes sought out the clock in the room and I cringed. Almost ten. I was a little surprised she waited as long as she had to call. "Sorry. Time got away from us."

"Joshy…never mind. Are you coming home tonight?" Her voice sounded resigned.

"Uh, no. Not tonight. Sam's brother showed up and we just need some us time."

"Have you not been getting that in the basement?"

I cringed again. Surely she couldn't be that obtuse. "We'll be back tomorrow. Tonight we need to focus on us." I stuck to my guns. I would not give in.

She said nothing for a moment, but finally sighed. "Fine. I'll see you tomorrow." She hung up before I could say anything else.

Falling onto the bed, I sat there frowning as I stared at the phone. There was nothing wrong with wanting to have some alone time with Sam—with no one else in the house. Was there? We didn't have much time before I had to leave, and add to that what happened today, we needed an escape, even if it was for only one night.

"Pizza's ordered." Sam called out before I saw his feet appear in my line of vision. The mattress sank beside me. "Everything okay?"

"Yeah."

"Want to talk about it?"

"I don't understand why it's so wrong for us to want one night away from her."

He wrapped one arm around my shoulders and drew me toward him, holding me tightly as the other one encircled me too. I could hear his heart beating in his chest, strong and sure.

"There isn't, but she is still your mother and she's still coming to terms with everything we've thrown at her." When he spoke, his beard rubbed the top of my head.

"My dad was so accepting of it, and didn't seem very surprised when I told him. My mom…it was a yelling match between her and Dad."

"I had the opposite."

My brow scrunched in confusion. I thought his family hadn't accepted his life choices. Pulling back, I waited for him to continue.

"My mom confronted me about it one day. She told me that she loved me no matter what and that I needed to be true to myself. My dad and brother on the other hand, have tried time and time again to make me straight since they found out. They've even gotten physical before."

I couldn't imagine. Even though my mother had a hard time accepting my sexuality, and I based that on her comments and actions, she'd never tried to beat the gayness out of me. "Damn," I whispered in complete shock.

We sat in silence for a short period of time before I asked, "Your mom passed when you were in college, right?"

"She did. I tried to conform one time to make my father happy, but I was miserable and I realized no matter what I did, I'd probably never win him over."

"So why was your brother here?"

"To bring me back home."

My head was swimming. "I thought…I mean…huh?"

"Doesn't make much sense, does it? My father has decided that he wants me to inherit the company. He's willing to forgive and forget, plus make me the CEO of his company, if I come home and marry the girl he's picked for me. Not happening. My brother was here to force the issue because he is a fucking puppet on a string for my father."

"Why the hell are they trying to force you to come back?" I blurted the words before I could think better of it. And then my mind grabbed hold of something else he said. "CEO?"

"My dad owns a small production company. Mainly commercials and stuff, but he's turned it into a successful business venture. My guess is that he thinks my brother is a complete moron and will run it into the ground. Probably true. Charles knows how to take orders, not give them."

"And why is he trying so hard to get you back?"

He hesitated and leaned forward, resting his elbows on his legs. "You have to understand, to me, when I lost my mom, I lost everyone in the family. After the hell my father and brother put me through, I don't consider them family. I've disowned them in a sense and have told them to do the same."

I placed my hand on his back and started rubbing. "Okay."

"Supposedly, my dad is dying. Not sure how true that is since they used the same ploy years ago. Turns out the doctors removed a precancerous mole on his face, and that was it. He thought he could use it to get what he wanted from me."

"Did it work?"

"For a few weeks, and then I walked away. It's one of the reasons I moved here. To get away from them all. Away from all the crazy."

"And then you ended up with me." I tried to joke with him, but it came out flat.

"Not a bad thing." He leaned back and gave me a quick, gentle peck. "I could say the same thing."

"I wanted you."

"That's a good thing since we're in the same boat." His words lacked…something. I knew he meant them, but they sounded downtrodden.

"Would you ever consider going back?"

"No. My father and brother are more strangers to me than family. Always have been."

"And if he is sick?" I didn't know how to help him. My mother and I hadn't been close, and she had her issues with me, but when I heard she was sick, I rushed home to check on her. Sam and his father were so far removed from each other, that they'd be better off not sharing the same DNA.

Sam shrugged. "It doesn't change anything. I'll never be what he wants me to be. I know it probably sounds callous of me, but I won't mourn him when he dies. I don't want to have anything to do with him."

"It's life. Sometimes it sucks, but there you have it. It's just life."

The heaviness of the conversation was broken when the doorbell rang. Saved by pizza.

When he left to get the food, I pulled on my jeans and swept my gaze around the room. I didn't know what I was looking for or what I expected. I saw two pictures that were on top of the dresser. One of a woman, who resembled Sam, and one of Sam and me at my graduation. I smiled. I was one of the two, and it had been added before I'd come back to town because I noticed it the first time we were together in here. That spoke volumes to me.

We were probably not done with his family, and I had a premonition that it would get worse before it got better, but we had each other. Even when we were separated, I knew he'd be thinking of me, much the same way he'd been since I left.

"Josh, are you coming out here?"

"Yeah. I was just getting my pants on," I told him when I walked into the living room.

"I wouldn't have minded you pants-less." He grinned, the spark back in his eyes.

"I would have. My luck, I would have dropped a slice in my lap." I shuddered.

Lifting an eyebrow in question, he pressed, "What happened?"

"Frat winter formal. There was an after party at someone's place because they had a pool. We changed into our swim suits and ordered pizza. A drunk girl grabbed a piece, stumbled, and dropped the hot slice, cheese side down on my lap."

He pressed his lips together, biting them.

"Go ahead and laugh. It's funny as shit, but one hell of a lesson to learn. No hot food near a naked or almost naked groin area." I waved my hand over my crotch, and he threw back his head and laughed louder than I can ever remember him doing. I liked the fact that I could do that for him.

"I don't remember seeing any permanent damage, but maybe I should inspect you more closely now that I know what I'm looking for."

I swallowed hard. Damn. The heat in his eyes made my body ignite.

"After food." He winked. Asshole.

"Tease." I harrumphed and plopped down on the couch, reaching for a slice of pepperoni pizza. I didn't taste a thing when I took a bite, my mind was too preoccupied with other things.

"No, a tease won't follow through. I have every intention of making sure everything is perfectly healthy," he announced as he sat next to me and bit into a slice loaded with pineapple and ham.

Oh hell. We didn't need pizza or sustenance. The human body could survive without food for a short period of time, so a few hours wouldn't kill us.

I dropped the pizza I'd been holding back into the box and climbed over him, straddling his lap. "Humans can go twenty-one days without food. I remember a certain biology teacher telling me that when I was in high school."

"It's a good little factoid that usually draws everyone's attention."

Grabbing his wrist, I took his pizza and leaned back to toss it into the box. "It is." I straightened up. "I think we can go a few more hours before food becomes a requirement."

"You think?"

"I know," I whispered before licking my lips, my eyes on his mouth. Unable to resist any longer, I smashed my mouth against his and moaned at the sensation.

I planned on seducing him, teaching him that he shouldn't tease me, but by the time we ended the kiss, we were both out of breath and I was no longer sure who was seducing who. I only knew I was hard as a rock and my body demanded release.

"Hold on to me," he ordered.

I did as I was told and his mouth slanted over mine again. I felt him stand, my body wrapped around his, holding on tightly as he carried me to the bedroom. Separating our lips, he dropped me on the bed where I bounced slightly. Scrambling backward, I waited for him.

He followed me onto the bed and reached for me. His hands fumbled with my jeans and he jerked them off quickly, throwing them behind him. I heard them hit something, and another noise told me whatever it was had fallen to the floor. I didn't care.

Once I was naked, he climbed off the bed to shed his own clothes before joining me again. I never took my eyes off of him, and while he made me wait, I wrapped my hand around my cock and started to pump it. He swallowed hard, and I licked my lips in anticipation.

He climbed over me, and I parted my legs for him. "Are you ready for dessert?" His smirk had me panting with desire.

I noticed that while his eyes remained locked on me, his hand felt around, searching for something. Biting my lower lip, I snickered and continued to jack myself off. "If you're looking for the lube, I suggest you try by my left knee. The only thing you're going to find on that side is a pile of sheets."

Rolling his eyes, his smile widened and when he found what he was searching for, he held it up. "Hah!"

"Are you going to hold it up like a trophy, or use it?" I mocked. Close to another orgasm, I had to stop my stroking or risk coming too soon.

My teasing had the desired effect. He flipped the lid, coating his fingers, and I closed my eyes anticipating his next move, groaning when I felt him circling my hole. I tried to impale myself, but he moved his finger back, returning it only when I settled down. This man was going to kill me with a pleasure-induced heart attack before it was my time to go, but it would be the perfect way to exit the world. Cause of death: orgasm.

His finger penetrated me and I hissed, pleasure flowing over my body. When he added a second finger and hit my pleasure spot, I screamed, demanding more. And he delivered. Sheathing his cock in a condom, he flipped me over onto my hands and knees, and rubbed his dick up and down my backside before pushing against my hole until the tip popped in.

"Oh fuck!" He always filled me and it always felt incredible, but for whatever reason, everything felt magnified this time.

Sam pressed forward until he seated himself all the way, and then pulled out slowly. He was doing it to drive me crazy, but I didn't want slow. I wanted hard and fast. I needed to be able to feel this later. "Sam, more!" I thrust my hips backward to meet his stroke.

I could hear him breathing erratically behind me, and his hands gripped my sides with brutal force. He felt as much as I did, and it still wasn't enough.

Growling, he moved his hands from where they sat on my hips to my shoulders. "I hope you're ready for me." His gravelly voice whispered close to my ear. I could feel the weight of him on my back.

"Always," I declared. At that point, I would have agreed to anything.

His dick started to slide out, stopping when only the tip remained, and just when I was about to beg him to move, he slammed forward, impaling himself to the hilt. But he didn't rest there. His thrusts became almost brutal; I accepted each and every single one of them.

"Grab your dick and stroke yourself," he ordered.

Without hesitation, I did as I was told, moving my hand in time with his thrusts, and periodically I would rub my hand over the sensitive tip. I was on a downward spiral, rushing toward my orgasm. Sam's thrusts became short and jerky, and then he quit moving, bellowing above me. That sound, that almost animalistic growl, had me spilling my own climax on the sheets beneath me and my hand.

Fuck it had felt good, but as he pulled out, I winced and fell onto my stomach, uncaring that I just landed in the pool of my own cum.

Sam fell on top of me and rolled to his side, keeping me close to him. "You okay?"

"Yeah." I couldn't possibly be required to say more than that. I was out of breath and still reeling from the amazing sex we'd just had.

My eyes were closing, and the bed shifted beside me. Sam had gotten out of bed. I tried to jump start my brain so I could ask why, but nothing currently worked. If I thought I was a boneless heap earlier, I was a puddle of goo now.

I wasn't sure how much time passed. It could have been a minute or a day as far as I was concerned, but eventually I felt the bed shift again. "Come on, Sleeping Beauty. I drew a bath for you."

"No." I couldn't move, didn't want to move.

"Yes. I have to change the sheets."

Cracking one eye open, I managed a small smile and croaked, "Don't care."

"You will in a bit." He chuckled.

"Doubtful."

He rolled his eyes as he shook his head, but the smile never left his face. This was the way I loved seeing him. Happy, without a care in the world. His brother's visit had dimmed that for both of us, but now that the spark was back, I didn't want it to disappear for even a second ever again.

"I can't move."

"You're high maintenance today."

"Complaining?"

"Nope. Enjoying it." His hand stroked my hair. "I like taking care of you."

"Me too. I like you taking care of me, and me taking care of you." I'd cooked for him a couple of times, and even though I was going to be leaving soon, I enjoyed the thought of doing this for him well into the future.

"We take care of each other?" His grin widened, showing off his white teeth. I was always mesmerized by the contrast of the light with his dark beard.

My sleepy grin intensified to match his. "Sounds good to me."

"Me too." He grabbed my arm and pulled me to the side of the bed. "Let's go before the water gets cold. I'm not carrying you this time."

"Don't want to go for three? You've already carried me twice. What's one more?"

"No."

"We're going to have to do something about keeping you in shape," I quipped. If anything, the man was in better shape than I was, and he was fourteen years older.

He opened his mouth and barked, "Ha!" Jerking me out of bed, he guided me to the bathroom, walking behind me with his hands on my shoulders. And then he helped me into the tub. I wasn't a big fan of baths, however, if he was willing to draw them for me, I believed I would quickly become a fan.

I laid my head back on the edge of the tub and sighed both with contentment and resignation. We probably weren't done with his family, my mother still had a ways to go, but we had each other. And even as my departure date grew ever closer, I chose to believe that the distance would not divide us.

Chapter 10

Samuel

I had never been more nervous to say goodbye to someone as I had been the morning after my brother's untimely visit, but I had to go to work and Josh had to go home. My boyfriend seemed to take everything in stride though, acting as if it was any other day and he had nothing to be concerned about. The thing was, I didn't trust Charles. I didn't think he would do anything to Josh or his family, or that he would physically hurt anyone, however, I honestly didn't know what he would do or how far he would be willing to go to fulfill my father's whims.

Neither my brother nor my father could be trusted.

Marcus Cayden earned the reputation of a shrewd businessman with good reason, but beyond that, he possessed a reputation for getting what he wanted when he wanted it. Charles followed him blindly, listening and obeying whenever an order was given.

With his uncanny ability to run a multi-million-dollar business, one would think he'd understand that attempting to strong arm his youngest son would net him zero. Even if he somehow managed to get me back home, I'd refuse to cooperate. If anything, I'd do everything I could to make his life a living hell.

And if he was dying—I didn't know if I could believe the news—nothing he did could force me to remain there. I wouldn't mourn his passing or feel sorry for him. I felt nothing for the man.

Sometimes I wasn't sure how he managed to run a business if he couldn't see beyond his own little world. To him, his sons were born to follow his orders, follow in his footsteps, and do what he told them to do.

Not me. I came out of the womb obstinate and disobeying every order he gave. As a child I got into trouble constantly. I remember being locked in my room for a week during the summer with only bread and water when I broke a genuine Tiffany lamp. My mother tried to lessen the severity of the punishment. It was changed from two weeks to one. But it wasn't so bad. She made sure I had books to read and snuck in some snacks here and there.

I was never sure why my mother stayed with my father, or how she fell in love with him, remaining completely in love with him until the day she died. He was not a lovable man. I remembered asking her one time, and she said, "Sometimes, it's what lies deep inside that's the true measure of someone." Deep inside I was sure my father was the same horrible man he portrayed on the outside, and when she passed away, he got worse.

The man was deluded if he thought I would drop everything and run off to California to fulfill whatever crazy plan he concocted. I'd run away and escaped, and I had no intention of going back. So sending Charles to me was a waste of time and money.

I loved my life. I loved teaching. To Marcus, teaching students was beneath him and should be beneath his sons as well. I loved Josh. My father hated the fact that I was gay. Basically, everything I was, my father loathed with a passion. And everything he hated, I was unwilling to change because that would mean being untrue to the man I strived to be.

Josh probably thought I'd lost my mind this morning when we left the house. I walked him to his car, checked the inside before I allowed him to get in, and then watched him drive away, refusing to take my eyes off of him until he disappeared in the distance. I did the same thing to my car before I unlocked it. If one thing appeared out of place, neither one of us was getting in our cars. I even got down on my stomach and looked underneath.

But I didn't limit my suspiciousness to my home, I carried it with me to school. At work, I scanned the halls, questioning anything that seemed out of place. I hardly left my classroom, and when I did, it was out of necessity. At baseball practice, I kept a firm grip on a bat the entire time, and then cut practice short. I'd turned into one of those paranoid people everyone laughs at in suspense or thriller type movies.

By the time I made it to Josh's house, I was exhausted. Stepping through the door, I was never so relieved to see Alice Dayton sitting on the couch, reading a newspaper. She was the lesser of two evils.

"Long day at school?" she asked, her eyes studying me as I slumped against the closed door.

"Something like that," I told her, scanning the room for my boyfriend.

"He went to the store for me."

"Oh." I tried not to sound disappointed, but considering she rolled her eyes, I knew I failed.

She folded the newspaper and set it down on the coffee table. Clasping her hands together in her lap, she leveled me with a stare. "Want to tell me what's going on?"

"Nothing."

"Josh said that your brother came for a visit. I didn't realize you had a brother."

"In all fairness, Alice, you didn't know much about me beyond the fact I was single and taught your son in school."

Sighing, she nodded. "You're right. Joshy made it sound as if your brother's visit wasn't exactly a good thing."

"It isn't. I don't get along with my family, and ever since my mother passed away, we've drifted further apart." That was the polite way of saying it at least.

"I see."

"My father and brother don't like the fact that I'm gay, and they've done what they could to convert me."

She gasped. The reaction surprised me since at one point, she tried to convince Josh to marry a woman. "I'm sorry."

I wondered if she was sorry for me, or if she was sorry for what she'd done to her own son. "My father, Marcus, has already picked out my bride. He thinks I need to give up teaching to marry her and follow in his footsteps." I didn't know why I was confessing to her, except I hoped that it would help her to understand Josh and what she'd been doing to him.

"But your students love you."

My lips lifted into a smile. "I love them too."

"What made you become a teacher?"

After dropping my bag by the hat rack next to the door, unsure of why I held onto it for so long after I reached the safety of the house, I walked over to the recliner and sat down. "I had a great science teacher that showed me there was more to the world than we could see. In a drop of water, there are hundreds of organisms. You can change the composition of something by adding a chemical, or even by adding heat. Everything she taught me, fascinated me. I found out the world was bigger than my family."

"She sounds like a wonderful teacher."

"She was."

"I know...I know you may not think it, but I do appreciate everything you did for Joshua."

"He was a good kid and a great student. He's grown into an amazing man."

"When..." She licked her lips as she wrung her hands. I could see the remnants of a white tissue in her hand that had been torn and strangled. "When did you become..." Her eyes darted around the room before returning to me. "...aware of him?"

This conversation had taken a turn and I had the feeling she was accusing me of being a pedophile or something. I squirmed in my seat, slightly uncomfortable with the new topic. "I realized I cared about him as more than a student sometime after he left." No need to be completely truthful with her. "After he came back, I realized I loved him."

Her head slowly bobbed up and down, but she no longer met my gaze. "Good. He deserves someone who will love him the way he should be loved. The way...the way I didn't."

How was I supposed to respond to this? I was stumped. I couldn't see her face clearly, but I saw how her shoulders trembled. I could feel the awkwardness growing between us, but that might have just been me. "You loved him. He knows that. If he didn't, he wouldn't have come all the way back here to check on you."

I heard her hiccup, and I sighed. "Alice," I began, stopping there because I had no fucking clue what to say. A week ago this woman threatened me with my job due to my relationship with her son, and now she had done a 180. I wasn't sure if I should trust it, or remain on guard.

And that's when I noticed, lying beside her feet on the ground were a couple of pages with some messy scrawl scribbled across what had probably once been pristine white paper. With time, it became yellowed across the edges and looked like it had been folded and refolded multiple times. A couple of small rips could be seen in the creases, and I saw a small hole in the middle of the top page. Studying the handwriting, it reminded me of Josh's, except this example was slightly neater.

"Did you know that when I met Josh's father, I was having lunch with some friends at Crown Candy in downtown? He walked up to me and introduced himself. At the time, I thought he was arrogant and annoying. And then he did something that shocked me. He told me that he was going to marry me some day. He was years older than me. Why would I marry someone like him? The next Sunday I went to church with my parents and there he was. He looked handsome in a suit. For six months, he only talked to me at church, and then finally, he asked my father if he could take me out to dinner. I was so shocked when my dad agreed to it."

I sat there and listened to her tale, somehow knowing she wasn't done even as she paused for a moment.

"Here was a man older than me asking if he could court me. My father liked him though, and I agreed to the date. He took me to a diner not far from my house. It's not there any longer. One of the many businesses I've seen disappear over the years. We had a good time and I agreed to another date. It didn't take long for me to realize that I loved him. When Richard asked me to marry him on our seventh date, he said, 'I told you that I was going to marry you, and I mean to keep my promise. Will you marry me, Alice?' He had a diamond ring and everything."

"And you said yes," I stated, assuming this was where she was going with this story, but what she said gob smacked me, and my jaw dropped open.

Her head still bent, her hands still wringing the tissue in her hands, she answered, "No, I didn't. I was afraid of our age difference and what that might mean for my future. He made good money and had a steady job, but I wanted to go to college, see Paris and Ireland, and I wanted to do it all without being tied to anyone."

This dumbfounded me. It wasn't like Richard had been ancient. If I remembered correctly, there had only been about a decade between them.

She nodded and finally lifted her eyes to mine. "I was terrified and let a lot of insecurities get the better of me. Plus my friends had been telling me that he was too old. I guess I'm still allowing others to influence me."

"What changed your mind about Richard?" I questioned, my voice gravelly and coming out more like a croak.

She didn't drop her gaze, but her eyes no longer saw me. They turned glassy, as if she was looking at something or someone else. Another time. A tiny smile appeared on her lips, and when she answered, her voice was filled with awe and wonderment. "He did. Two weeks after I turned down his proposal, he showed up at my house looking haggard. His face had a short beard, his clothes were dirty, and his hands were covered in black. My dad let him in after he banged on the door so hard that it made everything in the house rattle. One of the pictures that had been hanging on the wall, fell to the ground." She closed her eyes, her grin growing, and an expression of pure happiness lighting up her face made her look years younger. "He held up an envelope and shouted, 'I can't promise that we'll have all the money in the world, but I'll make sure your dreams come true.' I swear everyone on the block probably heard him. In the envelope were two plane tickets to Paris. That's where we went on our honeymoon."

Slowly, she opened her eyes and said, "I think that's where Joshua gets it. I've always been practical, and probably a little too worried about what others think. Funny, you'd think I would've learned my lesson after almost losing Richard. I was miserable those two weeks after I rejected him, and was on the verge of calling him multiple times, but always managed to talk myself out of it. Joshua is just like his father. He has dreams and has always known what he wanted. Even as a little boy. When he was two I took him to the store and he saw a ball he wanted. It was at the very bottom of this clear cylinder. He only wanted that one. I tried to give him the exact same one in a different color, but he wasn't having it. It had to be this particular yellow ball." She sniffled and laughed at the same time.

"That sounds like him. He's always been very determined." I could easily picture a young Josh demanding the yellow ball, nothing else placating him.

"When Richard told me Joshua was gay, at first I didn't want to believe it. Then there was the hurt of why would he tell Richard and not me. I'm his mother. And then the fear set in. How was I going to protect him if he was gay? The Catholic Church is against it. He can't be gay, because that would mean I would have to give up my son. But more than that, in this small town, if it got out that he was gay, I was afraid of what others would do to him. I'd heard stories and seen videos of people bullying and beating on people they thought were gay. It didn't have to be true. They got beat up because of assumptions and labels. I didn't want that for my son. I thought, surely, he's just confused and he'd grow out of it. When he didn't, I thought it was for the best when he left to go to college in Florida."

"That's why you acted the way you did."

"Yes." She sounded so meek and guilty, like someone had put her on the witness stand at her own murder trial, which I guessed she'd done to herself.

"Have you talked to him at all?"

"We haven't talked much since he was a boy, but he's not little any more. Somewhere I lost track of everything and he grew up into a man. After Richard died, I was lost and grieving. If I pushed everyone and everything away, I wouldn't have to feel that sort of pain when I lost someone close to me again. I even yelled at you when you tried to help him. My son suffered, and I regret that now."

It was only then that I noticed the door was cracked open, and I was pretty sure Josh stood on the other side listening to the conversation between his mother and I. "I'm not the expert when it comes to relationships with family, but maybe you should tell him."

"Maybe."

"Are you still worried about what people will say?"

She turned her head away from me, her shoulders hunching over, nodding. "I can't help it. I know it probably hurts him, but I think about that sort of thing. How will it look for my son to be dating a man? How will it look when people find out that I'm allowing him to date his former teacher?"

"I'd do it with or without your permission. Allowing me?" Josh announced his presence.

"Joshy, I didn't mean—" Alice tried to explain herself, but her son interrupted her.

"No." That word was harsh and I saw his mother flinch. "I don't want to hear it. I know you're scared of what'll happen to me. I get that, but Mom, it's a different world now. There are still assholes in it, but people are more accepting than they used to be. As for my relationship with Sam, it's no one's business. Not even yours."

Part of me felt like I should be defending her, however, I also agreed with him. Instead of saying anything, I sat back and let the two of them get everything out in the open. I'd talk to Josh later when we were alone, when it didn't seem like I was choosing her side over his. This wasn't about sides.

***

Joshua

I was seething. When I got home from the store, the last thing I expected was to hear Sam and my mother having a heart to heart. I stood outside and listened, feeling the iciness and irritation I'd directed at my mother start to melt away.

Until she got to the part about me dating men, and chose to say something about Sam.

It was none of her fucking business.

I stormed in with a little more gusto than I'd intended, but at that point, I was pissed off. It shouldn't matter whom I date as long as I'm fucking happy. Why couldn't she get that through her thick skull?

With each word I spat, she flinched, and I didn't stop. Thankfully, Sam didn't try to shut me up. This talk had been a long time in coming, and we had been skirting the issue trying to ignore it, or at least put it off indefinitely. It was time we quit sweeping it under the rug.

"I know you love me, otherwise you would've cut me out of your life completely after Dad died, but loving me and accepting me are two different things." My eyes shifted to Sam and I saw the almost imperceptible bob of his head. I wished I could have seen his face right then, but I was standing behind him and the only person I could see somewhat clearly was my mother. She had her head bowed, her hands clasping each other in her lap so tightly, they were probably screaming for circulation. Her eyes were squeezed shut, but I still noticed one single, solitary tear drift down her cheek.

I hurt her and I was probably a shithead for doing it, but I still charged full speed ahead. This was too important.

Taking a few more steps into the room, I stopped beside my lover and placed my hand on his broad shoulder, letting his heat and strength seep into my body. "Mom, I'm proud of who I am." I glanced down at Sam for a brief moment, a smile tugging at my lips. "And I'm proud of who I'm with. If you can't accept us...accept me without feeling ashamed, then I think it's time I leave until you can. I have to head back to Florida in a few days anyway."

Sam's muscles jumped as they tensed up under my hand. My leaving was inevitable, and this did not make anything easier. But I couldn't talk to him in front of my mother. This wasn't the time nor the place.

"Joshy—"

I interrupted her again. "Don't. I'm not a little kid anymore."

Sighing, I ran my hand through my hair, my fingers getting stuck on a knot and pulling out a few strands. I shook them off, and they glided to the floor.

She was finally looking at me, hopefully seeing me. Tears swam in her eyes, making them glisten. With the sunlight streaming in through the large window behind her, she appeared almost angelic, however, she was nowhere near heavenly in my eyes—not since my childhood. I was probably the biggest horse's ass for hurting my mother this way, but this was not something that could be ignored any longer. "Mom, I love you. I do. You were the one that taught me how to swim and ride a bike. You passed on your love of reading and your talent in the kitchen, but that was a long time ago. I grew up, and no matter how you feel about my life choices, they're my choices. If you want to be ashamed and worry about how others will judge you, then that's all on you. Hell, the neighbors have probably noticed Sam coming and going. I know Mrs. Byrd has, although that old nosey woman probably thinks that he's here for you." The last part was mumbled under my breath.

During my rant, her gaze had dropped back down to her lap and I saw a tear splash on her hand and roll down the side of it, leaving a wet trail. She did nothing to wipe it off. I heard her sniffle before she said anything. "Are you doing this to punish me?" Her words were barely audible.

My jaw dropped open. I twisted my head to see Sam's reaction to her question, asking myself if I heard her right, because surely she didn't ask if this was about her. "Excuse me?" I had to make certain.

She lifted her head, glaring at me through narrowed eyes. Her mouth was set in a thin, firm line. "Are you? Are you trying to punish me for not spending more time with you? Are you trying to get me back for ignoring you after your father died? I mean it would make sense that you would latch onto the one person who showed you any kind of affection during that difficult time in our lives."

I stood there unable to say anything. For that matter, I didn't think I blinked at all. Before I walked in here, she was telling Sam that I deserved someone to love me and now this. She was going to give me whiplash.

My fingers curled inward, pressing into Sam's shoulder a little tighter. His hand reached up to cover mine, lending me his silent support...either that or he was telling me to calm the fuck down. Normally, I went with the flow and let things roll off that I didn't like. Not now. Right now, I wanted to slap some sense into my mother and then march back out the front door. In that moment, if I had to make a decision about our relationship, I would've severed all ties with her.

"Alice, think before you speak," Sam warned her. He didn't sound malicious, but his voice held a distinct edge in his tone.

"This doesn't concern you," she huffed. All of their camaraderie disappeared.

"Mother…" I barked. If she continued in this manner, crossing that invisible line I'd laid down, she'd regret it. "Sam is trying to help you, I'd be careful. As for all of this, it very much concerns him because he and I are together. This is not some sort of fluke or transference. I've loved him since the moment I saw him. Nothing has changed nor will it change for me. That's it. Being with him would be the same as me being with a girl except for his gender." I glanced down, grinning. "And personally, I like him the way he is." His hand squeezed mine.

I forced my eyes away from him and back on my mother, my smile disappearing. "You need to figure out what matters most to you: me or others. In all honesty, I really thought that as long as I was happy, you'd be happy for me, but I guess I was wrong." After our conversation last week when she showed up unannounced at Sam's house, I assumed we were past this and had moved on, but that old adage about assuming appeared to be true.

I didn't think I'd ever felt more disappointed and disillusioned by my mother than I did today. She left me to my own devices after my father died, worked long hours, and tried to get me to date random girls, but this took the cake.

Swallowing hard, she cleared her throat and then clenched her jaw tightly. She sat there like a perfect, demure lady. Her back was ramrod straight, her hands were folded neatly in her lap—even if they were clenched together as if their very existence depended on it—and her feet were crossed at the ankles like she had been taught in debutante training. Apparently, that was something else that had stuck with her throughout the years.

I wasn't sure if I expected her to say something or not. She didn't, and in that deafening silence, I had my answer. "We'll be out of your way as soon as possible," I spoke through a clenched jaw.

Without waiting another second, I released Sam and walked away from her to my basement bedroom. Sam got up and followed closely behind me.

As I opened the door that led downstairs, I happened to glance at my mother one last time. She still sat on the couch, unmoving. She didn't even twitch. And in that moment, I'd never been more disappointed in her.

Neither Sam, nor I, said anything as I gathered up the things I would need to take with me. I still had so much junk here that I would actually need to get boxes and pack everything in order to move. That could be done a different day though, and if not, if she forbade me from ever coming back, there wasn't anything here I held so dear that I would regret leaving it behind. I'd taken all of that with me to college.

It was weird. I never planned on coming back here, and now that I had, I missed it more than when I left three years ago.

Sam took my bag from me and carried it up the stairs. I did one last sweep of the room to make sure I'd gotten all of the necessities before I followed him. My mother still sat in the same spot, in the same position, except tears flowed down her face, dripping onto her t-shirt to form a wet spot. I told myself not to go to her and not to give in.

"Mom?" She jumped slightly when I called out to her, but had no other reaction. Her eyes remained focused on the wall in front of her. "I think it's best if you don't try to contact me any longer. If you change your mind, call me, but if you can't accept me, I think this is for the best." My voice cracked. I think suffering through my finals at school were easier than saying this to the woman who gave birth to me.

Walking out of the house after that killed me. I met Sam by his truck and he asked, "Are you okay to drive?"

"Yeah." I actually wasn't sure if I was or not. My vision was clouded with unshed tears. Tears of disappointment, anger, hurt, and utter sadness because my mother cared less about her own son than other people's opinions.

Sam leaned forward and kissed my forehead, his beard tickling my nose. "I'll follow you to my house."

Another person in our situation might have broken up with me and tried to convince me to work it out with my mother. But Sam knew me better than anyone else, and he knew the situation. Even if he would've broken up with me for her sake, it wouldn't have changed a thing. This wasn't only about my relationship with Sam, it was about me choosing a man. Period.

He hopped in his truck and I turned to give my childhood home one last look. I could see my mother sitting on her couch, but instead of looking away, she peered out the window to the sidewalk.

All she had to do was tap on the window and tell me to come back. She didn't. She wouldn't. And until she made the decision to respect me, the door between us would remain closed.

Getting into my car, I pulled away. The tears that had been burning my eyes started to fall, and I forced myself not to look into the rearview mirror. I wouldn't see anything except Sam's truck behind me anyway.

To those who always told me life wasn't fair, you were right.

***

Samuel

I wished I could take away the pain and disappointment Josh felt. When he barged in, I never expected the little mother/son tête-à-tête to explode the way it had. The good news though was that I didn't think it was unsalvageable.

We parked side by side in my driveway and when he got out of his car, I grabbed him and hugged him, wrapping my arms around his shoulders. "You all right?"

"Honestly?" His arms loosely snaked around my waist and he buried his face in my neck.

"Hmm," I hummed in his ear, holding him a little tighter. This could have probably waited until we were inside, but I didn't want to wait to check on him. When he opened his car door and stood up, his face was red and his eyes were swollen. I'd noticed during the drive that he would periodically rub his eyes on his shoulders. It was hard knowing he was hurting and I couldn't fix it.

"I don't know."

I sighed. "Come on. Let's go inside and we can talk." As much as I didn't want to release him, we still had to unload my truck. On top of that, this was a conversation best done indoors.

The two of us grabbed the bags out of my truck and made our way inside. Yesterday, it was my brother. Today, it was his mother. Our families were out to separate us.

Josh dropped the bags he was carrying in the living room out of the way and shuffled over to the couch, falling face first, stretching out across it. His eyes were closed, but his features were set in a frown, and his bottom lip was caught in between his teeth.

"You going to give me some space to sit down, or am I supposed to sit somewhere else?" I inquired, attempting to keep my tone light. If he thought I would sit anywhere except next to him until after we had our discussion, he had another think coming.

He lifted his legs, allowing me enough space to sit on the end of the couch. "Gee, thanks. You're all heart."

"I do what I can." His smile didn't quite reach his eyes, but I could tell he tried.

As soon as I sat down, he dropped his legs into my lap. I placed one hand on his calf and one on one of the globes of his butt. Actually, I poked his ass a little before I flattened out my hand. "Want to talk about it?"

"I don't understand. We had this talk last week and I thought she was finally coming around, but then this. And it isn't like the neighbors haven't seen you coming and going this past week. They'd have to be fucking blind to miss it. Why does it matter so much to her? If it negatively impacted her life in some way, I might—not that I really do—understand a little, but this is just her being selfish." He spoke low and with a slight tremble.

"I wish I could make it better for you."

"It's not your job."

"I know, but I still hate seeing you hurt."

He slid his legs off of my lap and sat up. After scooting over, he leaned against my side, his head resting on my shoulder. I dislodged him when I lifted my arm to wrap around him, embracing him. I had to admit, I liked the way his head now rested more on my chest. "Sam, did you think about breaking up with me at any point today?"

"No," I told him truthfully. I'd had my doubts last week, and maybe they lingered even a few days ago, but after everything we'd been through in a short amount of time, my reservations were obliterated.

His head shifted so that he could look up at me awkwardly. "No?"

Shaking my head, I gave him a small kiss. "No. Your mother's issues and misgivings are about more than me and our relationship."

He snickered and grabbed my free hand, flipping it over and

studying it, following the lines on my palm. "I figured you'd say something like that."

I smiled hearing that, but didn't say anything. This was his time to talk.

It didn't take him long. "I just don't get what her issue is."

"She comes from a different generation than us. Before you, she probably hasn't been directly impacted when it comes to all this."

"You're probably right. I know that it's one of the things that caused the most fights between my dad and mom."

"What do you mean?"

"After he told her that I was gay, she would try to set me up with a girl or something, and my parents would get into a fight. He defended me each and every time. My mom always lived in denial. I mean…I guess after hearing everything she went on about today, I can sort of see things from her point of view, but that doesn't mean I agree with it."

"You don't have to agree with everything someone else believes or does, but you should see it from their perspective."

"Why won't she see this from my perspective?"

"She's scared."

Josh sat there silently for a few minutes, playing with my hand, turning it over and tracing the calluses and lines. Finally, he released a long breath. "I know." We sat quietly again until he asked, "Would you ever consider moving away from here?"

I shrugged, his head sliding a little. "Maybe, not sure."

"I have to go back."

"Yeah. It was no secret that you'd be going back to Florida. Just hard hearing that it's going to be so soon."

"You could come with me."

I chuckled, but it came out forced and tight. "I have class to teach, baseball to coach."

"What about next year?"

His idea wasn't new or original. I'd thought about moving to Florida multiple times over the course of the time we were apart, and now that we were together, the idea wormed its way into my head at least two or three times a day. It sounded easy, but it wasn't. It would require finding a job down in Tallahassee, turning in my notice here, and then selling my house, packing everything up, and finding a place to live down there. Not impossible, but not a decision to make on a whim. And considering I taught in Imperial, it didn't exactly attract teachers by the droves—not that that should be my concern or a reason to stay.

"Sam?"

"Hmm?"

Josh sat up, leaving the circle of my embrace. "You don't want to?"

"It's not that." When he pulled back, his hurt expression stabbed me in the gut like a knife.

"Then what is it?" he demanded. His emotions were still all over the place thanks to the run-in with his mother, and I needed to tread lightly.

"I want to. If it was just us, I'd do it in a heartbeat."

"It is."

"It isn't. I have a job here, responsibilities. I'd have to find a new job, quit my old job and hope they find someone who can take on both my science class and baseball, do something with my house, move, find a place to live down there…it's not something to make a snap decision about." Plus, the thought of running into someone that Josh slept with was not appealing in the least. With him, I'd discovered I had a jealous side. And knowing he's friends with some of his fuck buddies, made it that much worse. But then I wondered if it was worse to see them or to be here and think about him being there, surrounded by them, without me. Neither were appealing.

He tilted his head back too. "If all of that could be done, would you?"

I knew what he was getting at. "Yeah, I'd move to be closer to you since you'd have a better chance at getting a job down there than up here."

"Not to mention I have to work on my Masters."

"True."

"So, I'd be in Florida for a while longer."

Grinning, I fell to the side, resting my forehead against his temple. "We'll see." I'd thought long and hard about our relationship, and while I firmly believed he was it for me, I still thought we should move slowly.

A smile lifted the corners of his mouth and he turned his head, but before we could press our lips together, someone began knocking at my door. Correction, they were pounding so hard, I feared they'd break it down. Growling, I gave him a quick peck and ran to my door before it caved under the pressure.

Swinging the door open, I almost shut it immediately, right in my brother's face. He shoved his shoulders into the door frame before I could, though. "What?" I snapped. We'd already dealt with Alice, I didn't want to deal with my brother too.

"I have something to discuss with you." His condescending tone grated on my nerves and tempted me to punch him.

Crossing my arms over my chest, I blocked his entrance when he tried to take a step inside. "Whatever you have to say can be said right there."

"This is a business matter." He attempted to step forward again, but my body prevented him from doing so.

"What?" I snarled, ready to break someone's neck, and I'd relish snapping his with my bare hands.

He faltered slightly and took a step backward and tripping, running into the wall beside him. "I thought...I had to tell you..." he stammered.

"Spit it out already!"

"Father is insistent that you come home. He is willing to give the hoodlum hanging out here money for his education and—"

"You can tell dear old dad to shove his check, his bank accounts, and his business up his ass. I'm not for sale and neither is Sam," Josh sneered, his arms folded over his chest. He'd approached when Charles refused to leave.

"I haven't discussed an amount—"

"Don't care. On top of that, Sam doesn't want to go back."

Charles ignored Josh and looked at me. "He said as long as you keep your trysts discreet, you can marry the girl of his choosing and still have your affairs, but you must be cautious and no one can find out what you are doing behind closed doors."

"No deal. You're under some delusion that I want men. I don't. I only want one man and this is him. I'm not going to marry anyone Father picked out."

"You can't possibly mean—"

This time it was my turn to interrupt Charles. "I do. Now I suggest you leave before I call the police."

I slammed the door in his face. On the other side, I could hear his screams, but they soon faded away.

"Think he'll come back?" Josh's gaze was locked on the door.

"Probably."

"You could move and not tell him where you went. Live off the grid in Florida and make it harder to find you."

Throwing back my head, I laughed. Josh was relentless, and I wouldn't have him any other way.

Chapter 11

Joshua

Other than Sam leaving for work, our last few days were spent together. If only I didn't have my life in Florida. A job I could leave and not think twice about, but I also had my internship and school. This was my dream though, and Sam supported me. He had ever since I made the decision to attend school in Florida.

I didn't want to leave him. We'd just found each other and now we were saying goodbye. My anxiety had been building and now the night before we had to say goodbye, I couldn't calm down. I constantly rubbed my hands on my pants and couldn't sit still. As soon as I sat down, I'd get up and start pacing. More than once, Sam had to try and calm me down, but nothing worked.

That night, instead of going out to dinner, Sam cooked. A pasta dish…maybe. In truth, I barely tasted it and had been cleaning the kitchen for the past forty minutes, wiping down the same counter a dozen times.

It was more than leaving or being separated from Sam that bothered me. His brother hadn't shown up again, but Charles hadn't given up either. And the only reason he stayed away was probably because he was afraid Sam would kick his ass. We didn't see him, but he called constantly over the past three days. After he left on Monday, we'd received at least a dozen phone calls.

And then there was my mother. I hadn't heard from her since we left her alone on Monday. Yes, I told her that I didn't want to talk until she could accept me, but I really believed she'd be calling within a day or two. Too bad Charles couldn't afford us the same courtesy as Mom.

But more than anything, I didn't want to leave without Sam beside me. I'd done it almost three years ago out of necessity, thinking I'd never see him again. Our situation was different now. We were together.

"Josh, you're going to wipe a hole in my countertop." I felt my lover's arms snake around me from behind and grab the sponge out of my hands, tossing it the short distance to the sink. His lips pressed against the back of my neck and I closed my eyes, my body trembling. No one could turn me on the way he could. For that matter, I'd never loved anyone the way I loved Sam. He was my everything.

"Maybe I could postpone my trip a couple more days." I'd tried suggesting it before, but I'd quickly realized it was impossible. My boss had called me and he desperately needed help at the restaurant I waited tables at part-time. And on top of that, they'd moved up the timeframe for the study I had planned assisting with by a week. If I still wanted to intern and help tag marine life, I had to get back.

He leaned his forehead against the back of my head, and I felt him shake it back and forth. "You know that won't work."

"I know."

"We talked about this. I'll come down after school is done here and visit Tallahassee."

"And you're sure your friend will let you use his house?" Surprisingly, one of Sam's friends called to chat and Sam mentioned visiting me in Florida. The friend immediately offered Sam his vacation home, and my boyfriend took him up on the offer. It almost seemed too neat, too perfect, and after everything we'd endured with Charles this week, I didn't trust anything.

I tried to question Sam and share my concerns about it all, but he told me he and his friend talk every couple of weeks and it was about time for one of them to call the other. Fine. If he wasn't going to find it suspicious, then I wouldn't…like hell I wouldn't. I didn't trust it, but I prayed I was wrong.

"I'm positive. He is going to have the groundskeeper who takes care of the property meet me and give me the keys. I'll have use of the house the whole summer if I want it."

"You could make it longer," I muttered. His sigh blew across my neck and I slowly turned around in his arms to look him in the eye. "Sorry. I guess I'm not ready to say goodbye."

"Me either." His hands grabbed my face and tilted my head to the side.

A moment later, his lips descended onto mine and all other thoughts were pushed away. They still sat at the back of my mind trying to get my attention, nagging me, and reminding me of what would happen in the morning, but I could ignore them while Sam licked my lips and wrestled with my tongue.

Throwing myself into the kiss, I wrapped my arms around his waist, squeezing him as tightly as I could, taking comfort in such a simple act.

Between us, both of our dicks started to get hard, and when he twisted his hips slightly, my breath caught. "Again," I breathed.

He granted my request and rubbed his tented length against mine.

Holy fuck that felt good. We'd had sex in almost every room of this house, wanting to make as many memories as possible. It'd become a mission of ours, and we had succeeded in marking all of the rooms except the basement and the back patio. We'd done hard and fast, and sweet and slow. I was a fan of it all. As long as Sam was my partner, I couldn't get enough.

He ended the kiss, leaving both of us out of breath, and pressed our foreheads together. "I promise. We'll work this out."

"I believe you, but…" I dropped what I planned to say. Slowly, I opened my eyes, staring into his hazel eyes. Right now they had more gold and green floating around in their depths. When he was angry at Charles on Monday, I noticed they got darker with more copper and brown. This, though, this eye color was for me.

"But it's still going to suck," he finished for me. I nodded, rubbing our heads together.

I snorted. "Something like that."

Pushing him away slightly, I could see the same sadness I felt mirrored in his eyes, on his face. The smile he'd plastered on his face didn't make the corners of his eyes crinkle like a real smile did. He stared unblinkingly at me, as if memorizing everything about me. I wanted to do the same, afraid I would miss something major.

"We'll make this work," he reassured me.

I believed him, I just hated parting ways. Not to mention, everything else that compounded the issue. 'Please let us be okay,' I silently pleaded.

"Josh."

"What?"

"It'll be fine. We'll talk every day, and—"

"You'll be out my way soon enough," I interrupted.

His breath escaped like a balloon with a slow leak. My harping probably made it all the more difficult for us.

"Sorry," I told him softly.

"Me too. I wish it was different, but for now, this is how we have to do things. Eventually…" He smirked. "If you're good, we'll live in the same city."

I bit my lip so that I wouldn't laugh, and failed, and guffawed even louder when he joined me. This time the creases by his eyes did appear. This was a real one. We both hated what tomorrow brought and hated being apart from each other, but for now, this was our life. We'd make it work.

***

Samuel

Goodbyes sucked. Saying goodbye to Josh sucked even more. The day he appeared in his mother's house to check on her, I somehow knew my life was about to be irrevocably changed forever, and I'd been right. I couldn't imagine not having him at my side now, and it'd only been two weeks.

We'd gone from nothing to everything in the blink of an eye, something neither of us counted on; and yet, we wouldn't change a thing. Unless you included my brother and his mom. Those two made us want to bang our heads against the wall. His mother hadn't called him, but Charles called me on a daily basis…multiple times a day. I'd blocked his number on my cell phone, and he called me at work. I informed him never to call me there, and he called the home phone. Finally, my dear brother had been blocked on all of the phones I owned or had access to.

Josh's idea of moving to Florida without telling anyone was becoming more and more appealing. I'd even started perusing websites for teaching positions available in Tallahassee without telling him. I didn't want to get his hopes up and have to dash them in the next breath.

Tonight, I watched and studied everything he did, the different expressions he made, committing them to memory. When he got nervous, he would chew on his lip. And when he got pissed off or worried, he tried to keep his expression blank, which he typically failed at. His brows would draw closer together and his eyes became slits as he narrowed them. It was the first clue that something was bothering him tonight—besides the face he had wiped the same space multiple times. I didn't think it could

130

get any cleaner than it was.

At minimum, we would be apart for a little over a month. Graduation was still a month away, and then I had to wrap up everything at school. Thankfully, I hadn't volunteered to teach summer school this year and could leave after that about a week after the school year ended, unless the baseball team advanced through the championship level to state. With the way they were playing, it was a definite possibility, and I was the horrible coach that crossed my fingers and hoped they lost so that they didn't keep me from Florida.

We'd discussed everything and had a solid plan about what we were going to do, but that didn't take away the anxiousness. We were both affected by it. As I was trying to reassure him, I also tried to reassure myself. I wasn't stupid. Too many things could go wrong, too many hidden variables. If $A+B+C=D$, C was missing.

Tomorrow would come soon enough.

We still had tonight and I didn't want to waste it thinking about something we couldn't change. Reaching up, I slid my hand behind his neck, my thumb resting on his chin to tilt his head up. His hair fell back slightly, a few strands still clinging to his forehead and eyelashes. Why I thought I could forget him, I would never understand because being with him, even as short as our time together had been, showed me how much I'd been missing.

Too much.

Josh made life more interesting, fuller, and I coveted it. All of the arguments I'd had before, were thrown out the window the moment he stepped into his mother's house and unceremoniously dropped his bag. He was mine, and I was his. Nothing could come between us.

I hoped.

I prayed.

I worried.

God, it bothered me that I didn't have more information on the stupid "C" variable! Whatever laid before us, we'd either make it through together, or it would break us apart.

Chapter 12

Joshua

Sam's alarm woke us up before the sun peeked above the horizon, and I was not a morning person, but knowing this was our last morning together for a while helped wake me up. He was wrapped around me, spooning me, and holding me tightly against him. We were both naked since we had fallen into an exhausted sleep, worn out from trying to imprint ourselves on each other's bodies.

The warmth of his chest left my back momentarily, and I heard a loud crack. The bang reminded me of a firework exploding, but it was merely his fist hitting the clock forcefully. I snorted.

"Too damn early. Five more minutes," Sam grumbled, wrapping me in his embrace once again, holding me like an anaconda with its prey. Only he wasn't about to devour me, not for food. And if he kept sleeping, not for anything else either.

But he felt incredible behind me, his warmth seeping into every cell of my body, and then as he requested, we both went back to sleep.

And overslept.

An incessant loud ringing dragged us out of dreamland. Sam reached behind him and banged his alarm clock again, but it didn't shut up. Slowly, we both realized that somewhere on the floor one of our cell phones was crying out to be answered.

Mumbling with frustration, I left my comfortable cocoon and tried to find the offending device while still half asleep before it went to voicemail. No luck. I finally found the culprit—my phone—and sucked in a breath when I noticed the time. Forget the missed call, Sam had to be at school in five minutes for first period. Our chance at a long, lazy goodbye had disappeared as we slept.

"Shit! Sam! Wake up." I shook his shoulder as I unlocked my phone to see who called me. When I felt no movement beside me, I whipped my head around to look at him and almost laughed. He'd placed a pillow over his head and was holding it there with his fist. "Sam, it's 8:25. Class starts in five minutes." I shook him again and this time he heard me.

Bolting upright, he rubbed his face with his hand and glanced at me with one eye, his other remaining closed. His brown hair was curly this morning and sticking up in different directions. I showed him my phone and his eyes widened. "Crap." I didn't think I'd ever seen him move so quickly, running out of the room with his dick swinging side to side.

A few minutes later, he was walking back in the room talking on his cell phone, and I had to hold a hand over my mouth to keep from being too loud. I only heard his side of the conversation, but that was enough. "Sorry about this, Chris. I don't know what happened. All of the clocks in my house are blinking like I lost power. Yeah, I know, it's the weirdest thing. And because of that, my damn alarm never went off." He made the impression that he was truly put out and upset about this lack of alarm. "I'm hopping in the shower now and should be at school by second period. So if you can get someone to cover me for first period, I'll make it to the rest of my classes. Yeah. Thanks." He hung up the phone and threw it on the table closest to me.

I bit the inside of my cheek so that I wouldn't laugh out loud, but as soon as the call disconnected, I fell backward, my hands holding my stomach as I curled in on myself.

"It's not that funny."

"Yes, it is. You just lied to the principal," I chortled when I managed to regain at least some of my composure.

"What was I supposed to say? Sorry, Chris, but I was up with my lover until after two in the morning and the alarm did go off, but since I wanted to snuggle and sleep a little longer, I ignored it." His face burned bright red and he rubbed the back of his neck, but his upturned lips told me he thought it was humorous too.

Our amusement was short lived however, and we sobered quickly. This was it. Once we got dressed and said goodbye, this would be it for at least a month, maybe more. We no longer had time for a long, leisurely goodbye. Sam had less than an hour to get ready and get to the school. In a weird way, it made things a little easier. We couldn't linger, stretching it out, agonizing over our parting. This way, it was like ripping off a Band-Aid: quick, and the pain would be minimal. That was what people said, but people were full of shit. It still hurt. That said, maybe there was some wisdom in that advice.

I sat up, unable to meet his eyes, instead looking at the window. This place felt more like home than anywhere else I'd lived, and it was because of the man standing in front of me.

"Come shower with me?" He held out his hand, and I took it, refusing to miss even one second with him in our limited remaining time together.

Nothing else was said during our shower. We periodically kissed, washing each other's bodies. I wanted to remember it all, and when he slid into me for one last time together, I closed my eyes and tried to commit it all to memory. The way his cock filled and stretched me. The way his hand felt as it wrapped around my dick and pumped it, the calluses creating an erotic friction not even my own hand had managed to do. And the way he breathed against my neck and ear, frantic, as if he was unable to catch his breath, groaning when he climaxed at the same time as me. I wanted to be able to recall it all with clarity later.

We didn't have much time, him less than me, and after our elongated shower, we had to move at a faster pace, but it had been worth every second of it. I barely felt the towel that passed over my body to dry it off. I was too focused on him and watching him dry his own body.

After that, everything moved by in a blur. We got dressed, made toast for breakfast, and then we grabbed our stuff. All too soon, we were standing by the front door about to temporarily walk out of each other's lives.

We stood there, reluctant to say goodbye. I shuffled from foot to foot without saying anything, my eyes stinging. I blinked quickly so that I wouldn't cry like a girl, but my eyes were damn traitors and filled with liquid. Thankfully, nothing spilled…yet.

Sam pressed his lips together, not saying anything. He had to go, and yet he lingered. He sniffled like he had a cold and cleared his throat. "I…uh…I have to go."

"I know." We both sounded pathetic.

His hand cupped my jaw and turned my face upward. I reminded myself that I was not allowed to cry. If they had to fall, though, the tears should wait until I was in my car and Sam had driven away.

Brushing his thumb across my cheek and then my lips, he said, "Call me when you stop…any time you stop."

"I will."

"This isn't goodbye, it's I'll see you when I see you. Eventually."

"You quoting a movie or something?"

"Not sure."

His words made me laugh and sniffle at the same time. "So…see you later?" My hands were fisted at my sides, my fingernails digging into the skin.

"You'll see me soon, and we're going to talk every day. Okay?" I wasn't sure who he was trying to reassure, me or him. He tried to grin, but it was forced. There was no sparkle in his eyes, no lines could be seen on his face like when he really smiled.

I hated goodbyes, but saying goodbye to the man I loved was hell. Nodding was the only way I could answer him. If I said anything, I'd cry. And seeing him struggling as much as me, twisted my gut, torturing me.

He leaned closer and slanted his lips over mine, claiming my mouth one last time. I whimpered and my hands clasped the back of his shirt, mauling it. I didn't want it to end, but it did. Peering up to look at his face, his eyes were wet too, but like me, nothing had fallen. I reached up to play with his beard one last time. It felt as if I couldn't breathe and my heart ached.

"Soon." I squeezed out that one word past the lump in my throat.

"Soon," he promised.

One last kiss, and our bubble was broken when he opened the front door. He had to get to school and I had to get back to Florida.

I really didn't want to leave.

Chapter 13

Joshua

I sat in Sam's driveway and watched him pull out, wave at me, and drive away. And when he was gone, I stared at the last place I saw him, focusing on that one spot, my subconscious believing that if I willed it enough, he would suddenly appear again. It didn't work.

I couldn't even say how long I sat there in my car before the sound of my phone ringing shook me out of my trance. Hoping it was Sam, I answered it without checking the caller id, and then sagged in my seat with disappointment when I heard my mother's voice on the other end. I should've been happy, but she wasn't my boyfriend.

"Josh?" It sounded odd to have her use my name like that.

Clearing my throat, I answered, "Hi, Mom."

"Hi. I was thinking, hoping maybe, that you and I could talk before you left town." Her voice had a tremble in it and was a higher pitch than normal.

"Are you at home?"

"No, work. I was feeling better, so I came back to work on Wednesday. How about tonight or—"

I cut her off. "I'm actually on the way out of town right now. I have to get back to work and they moved up my internship by a week. So it's time I left." And quite honestly, I can't go through another goodbye with Sam. As much as I don't want to leave, that would be even harder, I thought to myself, but allowed that to remain unspoken.

"Oh, I see." I waited for her to continue because I wasn't sure how to respond to that. "Can you meet me for coffee now?"

"Sure, Mom. I'll meet you at your office in about forty minutes."

"Okay. Uh…bye."

"Bye." We hung up, and I had to admit, I was curious about what she wanted to say. She hadn't contacted me all week, and I'd told her that I didn't want to hear from her until she could accept me and my choices.

136

However, I wouldn't rule it out that this was a formality to say one last goodbye to her son.

On the way to her office, I blared the radio at an almost deafening volume. The tears had disappeared before my mother's call, and I didn't want to think about Sam. Music could either soothe the soul, or pour salt in a wound. For me, it was both. In each song, I could see a little of Sam in the lyrics, which brought to mind good memories. At the same time, thinking about my lover made me miss him, and I was hard pressed not to turn my car around and drive to the school.

As I exited, I saw the infamous St. Louis Arch on my right. I remembered when my parents took me there as a little boy and we rode up to the top so we could look out across the whole city. On one side sat St. Louis, Missouri, and the other St. Louis, Illinois, separated by the Mississippi River. I think that was one of the last family outings we did together. After that my dad lost his job and my mom went to work.

I hated downtown. It was always crowded, and with all the construction, it was hard to tell which roads went which way. I got turned around multiple times and almost hit two pedestrians. In my defense, they decided they were immortal and could survive being hit by a car when they chose not to check for oncoming traffic and cross in the middle of the street instead of at a crosswalk.

I couldn't remember the last time I'd been to my mother's office even before I left town, and it took me a little longer to find her building, but I eventually managed it. Pulling into the garage next to her office, I wound my way up the ramps until I found a place to park on the very last level.

I moved slowly on the staircase, in no rush to see my mother and making it to her office thirty minutes later than I initially said I'd be. She didn't call to check on me though, which could either be a sign she got busy, or a foretelling of what she had to tell me.

Walking up to the receptionist, I said, "I'm here to see Alice Dayton."

"And whom may I tell her is here?" She stared at me expectantly, a smile on her face.

"Her son, Josh."

Her smile broadened and she nodded. "Do you know where her office is?"

I looked to the left and saw a long hallway, then to the right, where I found another long hallway. I couldn't even remember where it was the last time I'd been here. Shaking my head, I answered, "Not at all."

She pointed to my right and directed, "All the way down, take the left in front of the breakroom, go until you hit the windows, turn right and there's her office."

"Uh, thanks. Down here, left, and then right. Right?"

"Yep, you got it."

I didn't have her same confidence, but before I could say anything, she answered the phone and ignored me. Following her directions, I walked right and found the breakroom. There I turned left, went to the windows, turned right, and like she had said, there was my mom's office. Her name was on a placard right outside the red wood door. In a sea of gray cubicles, she got a whole room to herself, away from the buzzing on the floor. How did anyone concentrate? I could hear phones ringing, dozens of people talking, and the clacking of typing. It would drive me crazy. Never before had I been so happy to be getting a degree in Marine Biology.

Knocking on her door, I waited until I heard, "Come in," on the other side. When she saw me, she held up one finger and waved me to sit down in one of the two chairs across from her. They were mustard yellow with armrests the same color wood as her door. I sat, and had to shift because it wasn't exactly the most comfortable chair I'd sat in, however it was a touch better than the plastic chairs in my classes.

I listened to her conversation, witnessing her in her element. She was confident and sure of herself, and talked to the person as if they were best friends, laughing and completely at ease. It was something I hadn't experienced much from her while growing up.

When she finally hung up, she met my gaze. Suddenly, the confident woman who'd been on the phone disappeared. She was replaced by someone who wasn't so sure of herself...or me. Her eyes darted from side to side and she squirmed in her chair while she folded and unfolded her hands.

"Mom?" I began, hoping it would jump start this conversation. I still had a long drive ahead of me and I didn't want to be here all day. I was just as nervous. My pits were pouring sweat and I fidgeted in my seat. Even my scalp felt prickly and damp, and I was sure my cheeks were flushed red.

She cleared her throat, her foot tapping under her desk. "This...I want...Do...Do you want to get some coffee?" she stammered.

I didn't blame her. I was anxious too. Glancing down at my watch, one I'd rubbed the watch face on like it was a magic lamp since sitting down, I cleared my throat. "Sure. I have time for coffee."

She sighed heavily in relief. We weren't very good at communicating, and this whole situation highlighted it. After I agreed, her whole countenance changed. She went from stiff and upright, to falling back in her chair, hand covering her mouth, and her eyes closing briefly. Apparently, she wasn't sure of what I would say, but I had agreed to meet with her for coffee over the phone, so this shouldn't have come as a huge shock.

We left her office and walked side by side. She introduced me to no one—not that I expected her to, but we may as well have been strangers instead of mother and son.

When we made it downstairs and to the coffee bar in the building, we ordered our drinks, and while I waited for them to be prepared, she picked a table away from everyone in a secluded corner that got less light than any other table in the establishment thanks to a burned-out bulb overhead. This was going to be as much fun as having a tooth extracted.

"Alice, Josh!" the barista shouted. Even though there were plenty of empty tables, a small crowd had formed around the pickup area, everyone waiting for the shot of caffeine that might help them get through the day.

I grabbed my iced tea and my mother's coffee and walked it over to the table. Suddenly, I had tunnel vision and the short jaunt seemed to take forever. When I finally sat down, I was out of breath, my skin was clammy, and I truly believed I was sweating buckets. Maybe I was about to have a heart attack at my young age.

"You okay?" she asked me.

Nodding, I told her, "Yeah. What did you need?" I breathed in through my nose and out through my mouth in an attempt to calm my racing heart. This was one of those moments I wanted Sam with me.

Her eyes darted from side to side again, as if this was a covert operation and she didn't want anyone to overhear what she had to say. Slowly, she lifted her cup to her lips and took a small sip before she set it down and once again checked her surroundings. Her eyes looked at everything except me, which only added to my own anxiety.

"Mom?" I pressed. This was getting ridiculous, and I almost laughed.

She jumped, jarring her coffee, which caused a couple of drops to escape the tiny hole in the lid. I stood up and grabbed a couple of napkins to give her a moment to gather her thoughts, however, her reaction made me fear the worst.

Sitting back down, I placed a napkin over the small mess and placed another one beside her, in case she needed it. I was tired and emotionally drained, and the small level of panic I felt mere moments ago had zapped me. "Mom, just talk to me," I begged.

Her lips parted slightly and she sighed, still unable to meet my gaze. Instead, she did what she did often and focused her gaze out a window. "When you left for college, I somehow knew you wouldn't come back to Missouri if you had a choice, and I was okay with that. It let me pretend things were good between us and that you were my perfect little boy again."

"Mom—"

Holding up her hand, she stopped me and finally met my gaze. "Please, don't interrupt me." She took a deep breath and continued, "I could pretend that everything was perfect. That when I got home, I wouldn't be going home to an empty house, that your father would be there with dinner on the table and a joke to make me laugh, and that..." She looked down, as if she lost the strength to hold herself up. When she spoke again, it was barely above a whisper. "I could pretend that you weren't gay. After your father told me that you had decided—"

"I didn't decide anything. I am gay. Period," I huffed, crossing my arms over my chest.

This time, she changed her words. "When you came out to your father and then he told me what was going on, I was scared for you and for us. What I told Samuel wasn't a lie. But I'll admit that I was also afraid of what others would say, how your choices would affect me. It was selfish of me."

Yeah, it was. I didn't say it, but I thought it.

Her head popped up. "I can tell what you're thinking, but that's fine. It's true." She took another deep breath. "When you came home to check on me, I thought I could keep pretending, but I never suspected that Samuel meant so much to you. I can tell he really cares about you if he is willing to put up with me. Looking at you together, I could see a lot of myself and your father in you two. It scared me. I didn't want you to have to suffer the way I did when I lost him."

"Loss is part of life, and I've already given him up and lost him once. I can't do it a second time. I had to take the chance since he was willing to take the chance on me," I defended myself and my relationship.

"I know it is, but when the person you've built your whole life around is suddenly gone, it will change you in ways I never thought possible. It isn't the same as losing a parent or friend."

"So you're telling me I should forgo love and lock myself in a lab my whole life? No, thank you."

"No!" She groaned in frustration and tried to run a hand through her hair, but it was pulled back into a tight bun and she wound up pulling some strands free of her neat coif, giving herself the look of someone who was about to turn into a mad scientist. Jekyll and Hyde had possibly taken residence across from me.

She gripped the edge of the table. "That's not what I'm saying," she snapped. Narrowing her eyes, she gave me the patented "mom look." Normally, it made me shrink within myself, but not this time. Either she was losing her touch, or I refused to cower this time. I went with the latter.

"Then what, Mom?" I demanded, grabbing my tea and taking a drink. After I'd sat down the first time, I forgot it was there. Now it served as nothing more than a prop. Something to grip and hold while I waited for my mother to continue her diatribe.

She shook her head and her shoulders slumped forward as her hand covered her mouth. "I…" Her voice was thick and she swallowed hard. "Did you know that you were the second baby your father and I had?"

This stumped me. I'd had no clue. Shaking my head, I spoke in a hushed tone, "No."

"The first one was born a month early and was a stillbirth. I have a locket somewhere in my jewelry box that has a lock of her hair. Melody Gabriella Dayton. You were born two years later. The whole time I was pregnant with you, we were afraid that the same thing was going to happen. We didn't even try for you. I didn't want another baby because of what happened the last time, but it happened and here you are. After you were born, we were over the moon. You were healthy, had all of your fingers and toes, and you were perfect. And when your father gave me the news, I lashed out. I hurt you. I know I did. I was just so scared."

I was getting frustrated myself, my anxiety churning in my stomach. "And now?"

"I know I did a lot of things that you don't agree with, probably even hate me for." She grew silent.

I wanted to yell at her to spit it out, instead, I took a long drink of my tea and bit the straw, grinding it between my molars.

Her fingers played with the lid on her coffee, a nail digging into the plastic. And then she spun the cup a little and put another indent across from the previous one. "I can't say that I'm over all of my prejudices and insecurities, or that I won't care what others have to say, but these last couple of days, knowing that you hated me, were almost as bad as losing your father."

"I don't hate you, Mom. I'm disappointed that you would choose someone else over me."

"I never meant to."

"Yes, you did. You meant to. At any point, you could have said fuck 'em like dad did and accepted me, but you couldn't."

"I was wrong," she quietly admitted, her voice catching. Her shoulders started to tremble and she picked up the spare napkin, using it to dab at her eyes.

If she expected me to correct her, she'd be waiting an eternity to hear those words from me. Rather than comforting her, I dug the knife in a little more. "You almost lost dad because you listened to your friends. I'm surprised you didn't learn your lesson with that."

She flinched, her chair scraping against the floor as it scooted back slightly with her movement. Her hands left her cup and fell limply into her lap. Her head was bowed again and I couldn't see her face, but I could hear her sniffles.

Maybe I should've felt guilty, but I didn't, and that probably made me a callous ass.

"You're right. There are a lot of things I should've learned, but didn't."

"So what's this meeting about?"

She lifted her chin. Tears streamed down her blotchy face. Her nose was running onto her lip and rather than wiping, she licked it away like a child. "I don't want to lose you, Joshy. I want another chance, if you'll let me. I know I have a lot to make up for, but I can't lose you like I lost your father."

I eyed her suspiciously. "You understand that I'm not changing, that Sam and I are still together and will continue to be together." She nodded. "You understand that at some point, I'm probably going to marry him?" It was what I wanted, but until we were both ready, I didn't want to count my chickens before they hatched—my father and his stupid sayings.

142

"I figured."

"And you're all right with having a son-in-law instead of a daughter-in-law?"

"I'm not saying everything is going to change overnight, but I am trying, Joshy."

I studied her for a moment. Tears still flowed freely down her face, but something about her had changed. Her shoulders no longer slumped and she looked more carefree than she had. This woman was my mother and I didn't want to kick her out of my life if she was willing to work on her issues.

I unfolded my arms and reached out to her side of the table with my hand upturned. When she placed her hand in mine, I gave it a small squeeze. "We can try."

No promises on something neither of us were sure could be fulfilled, but a hope and wish for tomorrow. It was a start, and I would take it with both hands and pray she could completely come around.

Chapter 14

Samuel

Three years ago today, or within a few days of the date, Josh confessed his feelings for me in a letter. It was a day that forever changed me and my life. And a little over a month ago, it changed again when he waltzed back home and claimed me as his. Everything felt surreal.

The funny thing was, since Josh's graduation confession, I'd gotten others from students. School girls who had a crush on their science teacher, but I didn't want any of them. Josh had been the only one that captivated me, and in another two weeks, I'd be heading down to Florida to see him and to interview for a new teaching position. I'd found a couple of leads and I couldn't wait to start a new life with him.

Or so I thought.

After Josh left, things became overly quiet, and that bothered me, keeping me on guard. My brother stopped trying to bug me and disappeared—hopefully he ran back home to my father—but I didn't trust it because this was Charles and my father, and I knew they were up to something. I just wasn't sure what it could be. Josh tried to tell me to think positive. He'd chosen to be delusional and pretended that they'd decided I wasn't worth the hassle, but that didn't fit their MO. They were typically relentless.

I didn't see it coming.

I got home from the graduation ceremony with the intent to shower and guzzle a cold beer before I talked to Josh later that night. All thoughts flew from my head when I pulled my mail out of the mailbox and found a wedding invitation addressed to me. Admittedly, my first thought was, "Oh how nice," but that only lasted until I opened it. Staring back at me was a wedding invitation to my wedding. Not only my wedding, but also some woman named Shelly Lee, who was probably an innocent pawn in all of this.

I expected my father to try something, but this was going too far. I saw red. Balling my hands into fists, I crumpled the invitation in my fist. I was breathing heavily through my mouth, picturing my father's neck in my hands as I squeezed tightly. Violence was wrong, but it was probably a good thing my father and brother lived in another state.

My body trembling, itching for a fight, I threw the invitation on the floor and tried to remember where I put my phone. This was going too far, and it was time I dealt with my family once and for all.

It took me couple of minutes to find the stupid cellphone in my pocket. I wasn't thinking, and honestly, the only way I finally found it was because it started to sing Take Me Out to the Ball Game. Josh was calling.

As soon as the phone was against my ear, I heard him say, "How was graduation?"

I didn't know what to say. I couldn't speak, I was so mad.

"Sam?"

I stood there, trying to calm down enough to talk to the one man that made sense in my life.

"Sam? Talk to me."

His voice was increasing in volume and octaves. He knew something was wrong, but I couldn't speak. Squeezing my eyes shut, I brought my free hand up—still fisted—and pressed it against my eye.

"Sam, you have to talk to me."

I heard echoes of his steps in the background and then the wind blowing. He was outside. Surely, he wasn't running down to his car to come back to Missouri. Maybe I should go out to California and deal with my family before I travelled to Florida. It'd postpone my trip, but the book could finally close on Marcus and Charles. Who was I kidding? My father wouldn't give up until he was in his grave.

"Josh," I croaked, my voice thick and forced.

"What's wrong? Is it my mother?" I could understand why he made that leap. Over the past few weeks, Alice had been making a conscious effort to change and called me periodically.

"No, it's—"

Josh cut me off. "Sam, why the hell do I have a wedding invitation for your wedding to someone else?"

"My father," was all I managed to force out.

"What the fuck?" Now he sounded more like me.

Taking a deep breath, I squeezed my eyes shut and tried to speak over him. He was grumbling into the phone, but I couldn't quite make out what he was saying. "I'm going to go out to California before I come see you."

That got his attention. "No, you're not."

"Josh, listen—"

"First, I'm not one of your students any longer, so don't try that to placate me and treat me as such. Secondly, no, that's probably what he wants and is expecting."

"I need—"

He interrupted again, determined not to allow me to have my say. "What you need to do is not give that asshole what he wants."

"If I go out there, it doesn't mean he can force me to do anything."

"True, but he can do something like have Charles marry her by proxy."

"I think you've either been watching too many movies or reading something I would prefer not knowing about. I don't even think that's legal any longer."

"Has your father always operated above the law?"

Josh had a good point. There were some occasions that I could recall in which my father walked that thin gray line.

My legs suddenly felt weak and I shuffled the five feet to the couch and collapsed. Sighing in resignation, I threw my hand over my eyes and asked, "What do you suggest?" I'd listen to what he had to say and then make my decision, but either way, my father would be confronted.

He said nothing for a moment and the wind blew into the phone. Suddenly, he blurted, "Marry me instead."

"What?" I didn't think I heard him right. I sat upright, knocking the table with my knee; the pain barely registered.

***

Joshua

Before I suggested it, I figured it would be met with some resistance

146

or disbelief. And I'd been right. I sort of hoped he'd—even if it was a longshot—say yes without thinking about his answer. I guessed we were at two different places in our relationship. It still didn't stop me from trying to explain my reasoning. "Look, it makes sense. If you're already married, he can't force you to marry anyone else, and if you married a man, it might send him over the edge and he'll stop fucking with your life."

I leaned against the wall, waiting anxiously for his answer. I'd been walking back to my apartment when I proposed, and now I stood there, holding my breath, waiting for him to say something...anything.

"Josh..." My name came across the phone line sounding irritated, kind of like a parent with a child, but we were a far cry from father and son. It hurt. I wouldn't say he broke my heart, but a small crack had formed.

"Sam, it doesn't have to be forever. Only until your father backs off." The uncertainty and pain I tried to hide from my voice, did not stay hidden and wove their way into my words, and a small tremor could be heard.

"Josh..." I heard him sigh.

"Don't. I don't need you to figure out the words to placate me, and really don't want to hear some lecture about the sanctity of marriage or that regardless of the reason, we shouldn't rush it. If you want to run off to California, good luck, I'll see you when you get here." I let my hurt and disappointment control everything I said and the tone I used, and when I finished, I disconnected the call and jogged to my apartment.

I was pissed off at him, his brother, his father, and quite honestly, every other asshole I'd ever encountered in my life. It was an all-encompassing fit of anger. My steps sounded heavy in the corridor, and I stomped on each step I climbed the stairs with as much force as I could muster. Even my poor door paid the price when I slammed it closed as hard as I could, making the pictures on the bookcases and the glasses by the sink rattle.

My breathing was heavy, not from exertion, but from being so upset. I shouldn't be. Logically, I understood that, but when feelings came into play, they made everything more complicated. If only I could get rid of these feelings...yeah, if I'd been able to do that, I'd have done it long before I graduated from high school. I couldn't.

Besides, it wasn't like I thought we were ready for marriage. Our relationship was new and we had a few things to work through, but I wanted to marry Sam. Only Sam. That said, if it helped his situation, then why not? We could figure out the rest later.

I could feel my phone buzzing in my hand. Someone, probably my boyfriend, had tried to call me at least three times in the last couple of minutes. I didn't want to talk to him right now. I needed to get my emotions under control and my head on straight before I spoke to him.

Running to my room, I changed out of my jeans and into my swimsuit. Maybe some laps would help me to settle down and clear my head.

***

Samuel

Josh suggested one of the most off the wall ideas and then hung up on me, and now, he refused to answer his phone. I called his mother and asked her to try, and she got the same response as I did.

I'd messed up and I wasn't sure how I did it.

Marriage to Josh. His idea had shocked the hell out of me, but not because it sounded like a harebrained scheme, but because it had been the last thing I expected. I'd thought about our future together countless times, and in my mind, we were together. When we were ready, one of us would propose—probably Josh given the way things were going in our relationship—and we'd tie the knot…when we were both living in the same city…when we'd been together longer than a couple of months…when…

I could give reason after reason as to why we shouldn't get married any time soon, but now that the idea had been planted, it had taken root. I thought about what he said, and I couldn't get the idea out of my head. It was stupid and liable to backfire. If Josh were standing next to me, it wouldn't seem so daunting and crazy.

But first I had to talk to him and he wasn't answering his damn phone.

After I called Alice, and before she called me back to tell me she couldn't get him on the line, I decided this was a conversation to have in person and not on the phone. Driving would take too long, but a plane could be there in under four hours. I was already in the car, speeding toward the airport with only two changes of clothes in a backpack with the essentials, when Alice called.

She made me feel like a bigger horse's ass than before. Not only had I hurt Josh, but I'd gotten his mother worked up and panicking. Way to go, Sam. Way to go.

"This isn't like him, Sam," she insisted while something in the background clicked, echoing throughout the truck's cabin. She was on hands free and her voice came through the radio.

"I know, but we had a little disagreement, so I'm sure he's probably just cooling his head."

"What did you fight about?" The clicking suddenly stopped. A pen perhaps?

"My family being dicks." Although the way I spoke, it made it sound as if I was asking her instead of telling.

"We already knew that, and Joshy chose to be with you anyway."

I laughed because it was true. As crass as it sounded, she was right. Shaking my head as I switched lanes to get around someone who chose to drive the speed limit instead of twenty over like me, I told Alice, "True, but my father decided to plan my wedding and sent the invitations out in the mail. I got mine today and apparently, so did Josh."

"Oh." She made the small word into a whole note in a concerto. And then she threw me for a loop and I almost crashed into the concrete barrier running down the middle of the highway separating I55 into north and south. "Maybe you two should get married." The same woman who turned a blind eye to her son's sexual orientation, who tried to pretend she lived in an alternate reality and threatened my job, just suggested her son and I get married.

"I'm sorry?" I squeaked. She had managed to surprise me more than my father's wedding invitation.

"It makes sense. If you two love each other and plan to spend your lives together, why not? I know Joshy loves you and one day wants to marry you, so why not take the leap now? You can make it legal and still take the relationship slow. Then when you're ready, you have a recommitment ceremony."

It was like she had it all planned out. For a brief moment, I questioned if this was all some sort of hallucination. "Alice? Do you

149

understand what you're saying?" It was my moral responsibility to ask her.

"I know it sounds weird coming from me, but it makes sense. Look, if you're already married, it's against the law to marry someone else. Your father can't legally make you marry anyone, but if he is willing to go this far, I wouldn't put it past him to coerce you into taking the leap down the aisle. With Josh at your side, you won't have to worry about marrying some strange woman—I'm assuming it's a woman?"

"It is," I answered in disbelief.

"Okay. Then you won't have to worry about marrying some strange woman because you'll already be married. Your father won't be able to dissolve it since gay marriage is recognized by the courts as a legal union. Plus, wouldn't you love to see the expression on your father's face when you show up to your wedding already married to Josh? You know it'll be worth it." She sounded giddy and diabolical, but I had to admit, that would be a sight to see. Hard to believe this bit of logic came from Josh's mother.

"Maybe," I said aloud, chuckling as I did. She had some good points. "What's in it for you?"

My words were more of a joke, but she gave me a sober answer. "My son gets to be happy. And if you two really love me, one day I might get grandchildren."

"Maybe," I repeated.

"Samuel, I want him to be happy. When I almost lost him, I realized that I was the one who had to bend, you know? If we didn't have a relationship, it was going to be my fault because I let my own selfishness get in the way. As a parent, you're supposed to be selfless and want what's best for your child. You want your child to be happy, and yet, I was the one causing a lot of hurt. It's a bitter pill to swallow. I'm not saying I'm completely all right with it all, but I'm trying. And if you two are going to be together, getting married to save your ass is a good plan. There are worse reasons to tie the knot."

"You're right."

"Does this mean you're going to ask him?"

"Mother and son must think alike. We got into a disagreement because he asked me earlier and I didn't answer him."

"Are you stupid?"

"I guess so." I forced a laugh.

She sat there in silence and the clicking resumed. Finally, she asked,

"What are you going to do to fix it?"

"I've called the principal and told him that a family emergency has come up and that I wasn't sure when I'd be back next week. He told me to take my time and to call him. Teachers are supposed to report to school for another week, but we don't have much to do."

"You're on your way to Florida?" she gasped.

"I'm on the 7:40 flight tonight."

"Are you going to make it?"

"I only have a carry-on. I'll make it." I had to make it. "Can you text me his address?"

"Yes. I'll find it and send it to you."

"Thanks, Alice."

"Fix this, Samuel," she ordered me as if I were one of her children.

"I'm going to."

"Good. He loves you, you know."

"I love him too." It was slightly awkward having this conversation with Josh's mother, who may very well become my mother-in-law.

The clicking sped up. "Just make sure you don't break his heart."

"I—" My radio screen announced that she had hung up the phone.

I never wanted to hurt Josh or break his heart. I knew I'd done just that today. It made me feel like a jerk, but I had every intention of making it up to him. I hoped he was ready for me, because now that the idea of marrying him had marinated, I planned to drag him down the aisle. Marrying Josh would be the greatest thing in the world. Seeing my father's face when I showed up with my new husband, our marriage certificate in hand, would be the cherry on top. "I'm coming, Josh."

Chapter 15

Samuel

It sounded simple enough: jump on a plane, land in Tallahassee, and once again all would be right with the world. I was naïve and stupid to think that anything about this would be easy.

There were no direct flights, so I landed in Atlanta and rushed to my connecting gate, only to find out the flight was slightly delayed and I would have to wait an additional forty minutes. I paced back and forth impatiently, annoying some of the other passengers to the point they would get up and sit somewhere as far away from me as possible. When they announced my flight, I practically ran down the boarding ramp to hop on a plane that would take me to Florida.

I arrived and the rental car company lost my reservation. On top of that, I never got a text from Josh's mother, so I had to call Alice and remind her of the address. She gave it to me and the rental company managed to find me something I could fit in that didn't resemble a clown car. It was still small, but I could deal with a Chevy Malibu more than a Chevy Spark.

I was finally on my way, and then my GPS lost the signal and I almost ended up in a marsh. Damn technology. I found my way back to the main road, got the GPS working, and managed to get to Josh's apartment complex without killing myself, which I truly believed was a feat in and of itself.

It took me thirty minutes of searching to find Josh's apartment, because for whatever reason, the numbers on the side of the building did not match the ones on the apartment doors…for any of the buildings. I think the only one that was accurate was the apartment office, which was darkened and locked up tight for the night. Considering it was well after midnight, it would have surprised me to see anyone in there.

Knocking on Josh's door, I waited for him or his roommate to answer. Nothing. I knocked again, placing my ear against the door to listen for any kind of noise. Silence. Was he asleep or not home? He'd been pissed earlier and he wasn't working tonight, which meant the possibilities were endless: party, bed, bar, etc.

And then in the distance, I thought I heard his laugh. I ran down the stairs, straining to listen, and rounded the corner. About five feet from me, I found my Josh shirtless with his arms wrapped around another man. Well, not completely wrapped. More like Josh was stumbling and the other guy was trying to help him walk. I still didn't like it.

"I'll take him," I stated.

"I don't think so," the other man scoffed.

Okay, it might have seemed weird for a strange guy to appear out of nowhere in the middle of the night and suddenly offer to take care of an obviously drunk man. No one in their right mind would say, "Here you go." I tried again, but this time I addressed my boyfriend, "Josh? Joshua, it's Sam."

His head swung from side to side and then lifted. He had a smile on his face, but his eyes were closed. "Sam? Sam's getting married and he doesn't want to marry me." His smile disappeared and his brow scrunched into a frown. He cracked one eye open and said, "Sam?" His eye closed and his head dropped.

"You're Sam?" My boyfriend's support pillar spoke up again.

"Yeah, and you are?" Since he wasn't going to give me my boyfriend willingly, I crossed my arms over my chest, flexing my muscles to make them appear larger.

Smirking, he shook his head. He looked handsome enough with his captivating blue eyes and short blond hair, but I preferred the rich brown eyes of Josh, and the wavy strands I could run my hands through. "You're definitely him. You look just like your pictures and you have a cocky attitude just like he said. I'm his friend Jacob."

For a friend, there was something intimate in the way he talked about Josh and how his right arm was wrapped around my boyfriend's waist, his hand resting on Josh's hip. He must have seen me staring because suddenly, the hand moved upward several inches. "Want to tell me what happened?" I asked, not so politely.

Jacob shrugged, but the damn smirk never left his face. I disliked him. "I guess you two had a fight and he went and did about a million laps in the lap pool on campus, and then we went out for a drink or ten."

"Ten?" This kid had poured ten drinks down my boyfriend's throat? Yes, I knew I was thinking irrationally, however, jealousy could be a bitch when she whispered in your ear.

"Relax, man. It was a figure of speech. He's only had four or five, but they were shots."

I willed myself to calm down, counting to ten a couple of times in my head, before I reached out and cupped Josh's cheek, lifting his head. My heart clenched when I felt wetness from more than just sweat. It was warm and humid, but only tears could explain the dampness on his face. "I'll, uh, I'll take him."

"I got him. I'll just put him to bed—"

I took a menacing step forward. This guy had to be stupid or something. It would be over my dead body before I let him put my boyfriend to bed. "No, Josh is my responsibility, I'll put him to bed."

"You don't have the key," Jacob challenged.

"And you do?"

"I have his keys. I snatched them while we were at the bar. Since his roommate is in Ohio visiting family, it was the only way to make sure I could get him home. His place is a lot closer than mine."

Hearing him speak so casually and talk about whose place was closer to the bar, made me seethe. I worked my head from side to side to try and loosen up my neck, making it crack and pop. My free hand, the one that wasn't holding onto Josh's face, opened and closed into a fist at my side repeatedly. Every muscle in my body was tight and ready to spring, ready to beat this guy into a pulp, but I refrained. "Let's get one thing straight," I sneered with my jaw clenched tightly, "Josh is mine, so whatever ideas you have about him, wash your mind with bleach and remove them. I'll take him and his keys, and I'll be the one putting him to bed. You can scurry away and leave him alone."

The idiot's smirk grew. "You going to marry him?"

This question threw me off kilter. "That doesn't concern you."

"Oh, but it does. You see, Josh here is one of my closest friends and I don't like to see him upset. He's been going on and on about how you don't want to marry him. So are you going to make an honest man of him?"

I didn't want to discuss this with a complete stranger before I talked to Josh. "I flew all the way from Missouri to talk to him."

"Not the answer I was looking for, but good enough." He snickered as he tossed me a set of keys. Swinging Josh's arm from around his neck, Jacob pushed my boyfriend toward me, spun around, and he spoke over his shoulder, "Don't hurt him like that again. He's loved you for a long time, which made relationships difficult for him. He's a good man and you won him long before he ever set foot on campus. Take care of him."

I easily caught Josh and held him upright. Jacob walked away, leaving me with my charge, but I had to wonder if he didn't have some sort of feelings for Josh as well. I almost felt bad for him...almost.

"Sam?" Josh breathed against my shoulder as I wrapped one of his arms around my neck as my left one snaked around his waist.

"Yeah, it's me." I kissed his temple and then slowly walked both of us toward the stairs.

It might have been easier to carry him, however, the stairs were a bit steep and if he woke up, I didn't want risk falling backward. This was the easiest way to get him home, but fuck, his dead weight was not easy to drag up a flight of stairs.

By the time we finally reached his apartment, I was out of breath and sweating like I'd just ran a marathon. I unlocked his door, and a burst of cool air greeted me. Sweet relief. I pulled him inside and walked down a short hallway. To the right was a small kitchen and straight in front of me was a living area. Across from the kitchen was one door and a second door was located in the living room. I assumed those were the bedrooms, but since I wasn't sure which one belonged to Josh, I laid him on the couch and covered him up with the blanket that had been rolled into a ball on the end.

My indecision caused this, but I hadn't been expecting him to simply blurt out that I needed to marry him over some strange woman. When I read the invitation, I had no intention of marrying anyone, and I certainly hadn't intentionally hurt him.

Sitting on the ground beside the couch, I leaned my head against the middle cushion. Close enough to him that I could touch his face and hair if I wanted, and far enough away that if he threw up, I was out of the target area.

I tilted my head back and watched him sleep, my hand reaching out of its own accord to rub a few strands of his hair between my fingers. Closing my eyes, my hand continued to play with his hair, waiting for him to wake up so I could take care of him.

***

I didn't remember falling asleep, but I must have because when I opened my eyes, the morning sun was peeking through the blinds in the living room.

For the first time since I deposited Josh on the couch, I really surveyed the apartment. It was small, with vinyl flooring that resembled hardwood in the living room. There was a small circular dining room table that looked overrun with two computers and a pile of text books. The kitchen was tiny and near the front door, but considering two college students lived here, it was big enough. There was a coffee table by the windows overlooking the balcony, an oversized yellow chair inches from the table with a round, orange ottoman in front of it, and the tan couch. That was about it for furnishings. And none of it matched, but again, I hadn't expected much from college students.

"Sam?" Josh's voice called out to me.

I turned and met his disbelieving gaze. He closed his eyes and opened them again, frowning. "I'm really here," I commented with a snicker, thinking he was trying to make sure I was real.

"I can see." He'd closed his eyes once again and flipped over to his back. "When did you get here?"

"Last night."

"You didn't have to. We're fine." If he was saying that in such a flat tone of voice with his eyes closed, not looking at me, then we were very much not fine.

"Josh."

"How long are you staying? When do you leave for California?"

"Josh."

"It's fine." He hefted himself into a sitting position and scooted to the other end of the couch. Standing on shaking legs, he staggered to the door in the living room and grabbed the doorknob. "I'm going to take a shower. Feel free to make yourself at home. There's drinks in the fridge, but not sure what we have as far as breakfast stuff. I'll be out in a few."

He wasn't letting me say anything, which irritated me. Jumping up from my position on the floor, I grabbed the door before it could close. "Josh, we need to talk."

"About what? If I made you feel guilty, I'm sorry. Can you get out so

156

that I can take a shower? If you need a shower or to use the bathroom, you'll have to use this one. My roommate is out of town, and locked his bedroom door."

"Why would he do that?"

Josh grinned. "He doesn't like my friend Jacob. Jacob's been known to go through my roommates drawers just to piss Gabe off."

"Somehow, I can picture Jacob doing that," I grumbled, rolling my eyes and shaking my head.

"You can?" His frown was back.

"Yes, while I was waiting for you, I thought I heard your voice. When I got down the stairs, I found Jacob dragging you home."

His eyes widened and he looked away. "Oh."

I didn't like the sound of that one meager word. "Josh, what happened between you and him?" In hindsight, this was probably not the best time to question him about Jacob.

He whipped his head around to glare at me with narrowed eyes, and swayed. I caught him before he could fall. "I'm fine." He tried to push me away.

"Josh, let me help. Do you feel sick?"

"Just a little dizzy."

"Then I'm not letting you take a shower alone."

"Why?"

"Because I don't want to have to take you for a set of stitches before I take you to the JP."

He froze, his breathing coming out harder, faster. His skin started to become flushed and I was worried that he was having some sort of reaction to all the alcohol he consumed the night before. Before I could ask if I needed to call 911, he asked, "What did you say?" His voice was soft and measured. Slowly, he met my gaze, his eyes narrowed.

In return, I smiled and kissed his warm cheek. "I'd rather take you to the JP than take you to the hospital. Did you know that since you're still considered a resident of Missouri—I am as well— we can go down, get a marriage license on Monday, and be married the same day? If you were a resident, we'd have to wait a few days, but the waiting period is waived since we aren't Florida residents yet."

"Yet?" He shook his head slightly as if trying to clear it.

"All that's required is for us to go down to the Leon County

157

Courthouse and get a marriage license."

"What?"

I didn't blame him for being unable to keep up. I showed up out of the blue, he's hungover, and I just unceremoniously announced that I planned on marrying him while I was there. Not my best moves.

Unable to stand still, I skirted past him and closed the toilet seat, giving him a place to sit. Once he sat down and I no longer had to worry about him face planting into one of the fixtures, I busied myself with small tasks. I turned on the water for him, pulled the towel off the towel rack, checked the temperature of the water, and while I did all of this, I rambled. "It's not that I didn't want to marry you before. I mean, yeah I thought it was really soon, but I don't want you to think I don't love you. I do."

"So you came here and announced you were going to take me to the Justice of the Peace to prove that you loved me?" Josh asked.

"No!" I rushed. I forced myself to stop and take a couple of deep breaths. Placing both hands on the sink, I leaned forward, staring at him through the mirror as he sat there looking at me expectantly. Our eyes met in the reflective surface. One of his brows was lifted, the other one I couldn't see because of the way his bangs fell over his face.

The shower beat down on the empty tub, steam filled the room and started to fog up the mirror, but we didn't break eye contact. "Josh, it's quick and I don't know. I always had it in my head that when I got married it would be to someone I was with two years, not two months— no matter the circumstances."

"But?" he prodded.

"But maybe you're right."

"Sam, we had a fight. You didn't have to come here—"

"Yes, I did." The mirror was now too steamed over to see him clearly, and for this, I needed to look him in the eye. I took in a couple more deep breaths and released them, although since I began to feel lightheaded, I suspected I was making myself hyperventilate more than breathing.

Spinning around, I explained myself, "Josh, your letter changed me, but even before that, you captivated me. I didn't think I'd see you again and when you showed up, I was shocked. I tried to fight the attraction, my feelings, your feelings…everything, and I lost. All of this bullshit with my father and my brother, I never wanted it to touch you, and yet, here

158

we are. I love you. When you suggested marriage, I really thought it was all too soon. I'm not going to lie, but the more I thought about it, the more I liked the idea. For your information, I have a couple of job interviews lined up here in Tallahassee. I also talked to your mother, who gave me an earful."

"She tell you not to marry me?" His words were full of trepidation and he continued to stare at me suspiciously. His eyes were still narrowed and his hands were holding up his head.

I chuckled nervously. "Surprisingly, no. At first, I didn't mention your proposal, but when I told her about the invitation, she told me to marry you. She suggested that it might be a nice feather in our caps to get married and show up to the wedding with our marriage certificate, knowing he can't do shit about it. Don't tell her, but picturing my father blowing a gasket when he hears we got married is kind of a nice visual."

"So you're marrying me for revenge?"

"No. We're not going to California, unless you want to. But I'm marrying you because I don't want anyone to separate us. I know you're it for me, for the rest of my life. And I hope you feel the same, because I don't think you would have proposed marriage if you didn't."

"You really want to marry me?" He tilted his head to the side, his frown increasing. The way he bit his lip and the shakiness in his voice made me feel guilty for ever causing him one iota of pain. He wanted to believe me, but wasn't quite sure he could.

I got down on one knee and rested my hands on his thighs. "I love you and I want to marry you. So what do you say? Will you marry me?"

A smile appeared on his soft, red lips. "On one condition."

"What's that?"

"We tell your father together. He needs to know he lost." I never thought Josh had a vindictive bone in his body, but he proved me wrong.

Throwing back my head, I laughed loudly. "Anything you want. Does that mean you're going to marry me?"

His smile was blinding. "Yeah."

I tried to kiss him, but he turned his head before our lips could meet. "Issues?"

"I drank too much last night, and I should brush my teeth," he muttered resting his forehead on my shoulder, turning it slightly into my neck so that I could feel his breath on my skin.

"You okay?"

"Relieved and hungover. I'll be fine. I think I drank too much vodka and not enough water."

"You know your shower water is probably cold now."

He chuckled. "Probably. What do you want to do while we wait for the water to get warm?" he asked breathlessly, kissing my neck where my beard stopped.

In response, my dick sprang to life. I'd never get enough of him, however, his health had to be my top priority. He'd been dizzy this morning and before we did anything, I had to make sure he was all right. Pulling back reluctantly, I told him, "You brush your teeth and I'm going to get my bag out of the car. I'll also check out the kitchen and see what you have, unless you want to go out to eat."

"When I asked what we could do, this isn't what I meant." He grinned.

I rolled my eyes. Damn, I wanted to fuck him, but there were other things that took precedence. "I know, and I'd love nothing more than to do that and more, but you were dizzy this morning. Let's get some food in you and then we can spend all weekend in bed if you want."

I headed for the bathroom door when he stopped me. "Sam?"

"Yeah?" I leaned against the door and waited for him to speak.

His smile had disappeared and now he was gnawing on his lip as if it was a meal in and of itself. "How long are you staying?"

"I'm flying back next week, packing more clothes, and then driving back down. I have a job interview in two weeks."

His smile had returned. "You've been plotting. How much did you pack?"

I chuckled and nodded. "Plotting a little, and only two changes of clothes. I was kind of in a rush to get here last night. Let me just say, being apart this past month wasn't any fun."

"Phone sex not good?" Josh teased, but he carefully rose to his feet and approached me. "It wasn't fun for me either."

It bothered me to see him moving so cautiously. I hoped food and lots of water would help him bounce back. I kissed the side of his head and hugged him tightly. This felt like home. Since he'd left, I moved around from room to room anxiously. It no longer felt right, but in his arms, his body pressed against mine, and him in the same room as me, everything realigned and fell back into place.

"Get ready and let me get my stuff. I never got the opportunity to change after graduation yesterday."

He breathed in deeply. "At least you don't stink."

One last kiss, this time on his neck, and I held him away from me and walked out of his bedroom. I didn't realize how good it was to be with him until all we had were facetime and phone calls. Being physically together was completely different, and felt more real.

When I had arrived the night before and had a hard time figuring out which building Josh lived in, I parked where I thought his building was, six buildings away, which equated to almost two blocks. I moved the car closer, slung my bag over my shoulder, and then ran back to the apartment. I didn't expect to see Jacob standing at the door, flirting with my boyfriend—no, Josh was my fiancé now—as he brushed his teeth and grunted in response to whatever Jacob said.

Approaching them, I cleared my throat, and fought the smile that threatened to appear on my lips when Josh's face lit up upon seeing me. "Jacob, right?" I attempted to sound polite, but based on the way Josh snorted, I wasn't sure I succeeded.

"That's right," Jacob answered. He tilted his head toward my fiancé and said, "I was just checking on the drunkard."

"I was only drunk because the bartender kept putting the shots in front of me." With a mouthful of toothpaste and spit, his defense sounded garbled and hard to understand, and he looked rabid with white foam around his mouth.

"Whatever. You didn't have to drink them." Jacob guffawed.

I still thought there was something too intimate about these two. Yes, it could be my jealousy talking, but I got the impression that there was something more between them at some point in their history. I also believed that whatever it was, ended before Josh came back to Missouri.

Josh disappeared into the apartment, and I took the opportunity to situate myself between him and Jacob, preventing the stranger from entering with a hand on his chest. "Thanks for coming over and checking on him. He's fine and we have a date this morning."

"Oh well, I don't want to intrude on a date." Jacob eyed me warily, glancing from my hand to my face, his grin never dropping. "You may want to be careful. Next time you fuck up, someone else could be waiting around ready to clean up your mess."

"What's that supposed to mean?" Josh demanded. He'd only been in the kitchen rinsing out his mouth.

"Nothing. But last night—" Jacob began.

"Last night I was upset and that was it. I knew Sam and I would work it out because we've waited too long to be together."

"It was always him, wasn't it?"

What the hell did that mean?

"Always."

Somehow, I found myself in the middle of a two-sided conversation, and I wasn't completely sure what was being discussed. I only knew that it had something to do with me.

Jacob exhaled loudly and nodded; the smile on his face had disappeared the moment Josh reappeared. "I'll see you Tuesday still?"

"Yeah, I'll be there."

With his shoulders hunched and his head bowed slightly, Jacob shuffled toward the stairs. If he looked back, we didn't see it because we shut the door.

The moment the latch caught after pushing the large metal door closed, he sagged against the wall. I rushed to him, concerned. "Josh?"

"I'm fine. Just tired. I should probably eat something."

I let him temporarily distract me from my questions. "Let me take a quick shower and get changed. I'll take you out for breakfast."

"Or we could forgo the shower and go through the drive-thru. That's kind of why they're there."

Rolling my eyes, I agreed. "Fine. Pick something and I'll go and get it."

"I'll come with you."

"You sure?"

"Yeah. I need some fresh air."

I led him out of the apartment and hovered next to him as he maneuvered the stairs. Falling into the passenger seat of my car, a thin sheen of sweat covered his face.

My worry only decreased when he ate everything he ordered as if it was the last meal on earth. Pancakes, eggs, sausage, and two breakfast burritos from McDonald's. Not the healthiest breakfast, but it was quick and close. Besides that, it was what he requested.

Breakfast reinvigorated him. His face had more color, and it probably also helped that he'd already downed four large glasses of water. He was going to be all right and I could stop hovering.

I waited until after breakfast before I asked, "Who's Jacob? And what's happening on Tuesday?"

Josh leaned forward to rest his elbows on his knees, and from where I sat next to him on the couch, leaning against the cushions, I could no longer see his face. My stomach felt like it dropped because he wasn't saying anything. "Josh?" I placed my hand on his back and rubbed.

Glancing over his shoulder at me, he finally explained, "I guess you can sort of call him an ex. He was one of my first friends on campus. At some point, we became friends with benefits."

I swallowed hard, moving my other hand to scratch my chest. I figured it had been something like that, but it goaded me to hear it confirmed. Josh had a past, I had a past, and I couldn't hold his against him. I shouldn't be jealous, but I was. I was jealous of everyone whom Josh had been with after he wrote out his confession to me. And this man acted like he only had to snap his fingers and Josh would come running. That made me furious.

"You knew I'd been with others," he spoke cautiously.

"I know."

"You have too."

"I know."

"You can't—"

"I'll be okay." I dropped my hand from his back and looked upwards.

The couch shifted next to me and then he straddled me. Grabbing my face in both of his hands, he met my eyes. "He doesn't mean anything to me besides friendship. When I was with him, I was thinking about you every time. He knows it. That's why he said what he did. Tuesday is our monthly meeting at the frat house. That's it. He means nothing and I haven't been with him since before I went back home. And it was horrible because I couldn't stop thinking about you and nothing happened. So, whatever is going on in that brain of yours, quit it."

At some point during his lecture, his hands started to rake through my beard. He had developed a habit of touching it when we were together in Missouri. It was not something I'd ever considered erotic, but with Josh, it had become a huge turn-on for me. In all fairness, there wasn't much he did that didn't get me hard in less than ten seconds, but who was I to complain?

"Sorry, I will." Which actually meant, I'd try to hide my jealousy around him, but I still didn't like Jacob.

***

Joshua

I wasn't fooled by this man or his words, but I could admit that it gave me a small thrill knowing he was jealous of Jacob, even if there was nothing to be jealous about. Jacob had more of a swimmer's body, clean shaven, and short blond hair. It had been longer before I'd gone to Missouri, however, due to some sort of prank that my roommate, Gabe, played on him involving gum, Jacob cut it.

Jacob was sexy, but I preferred someone who could probably bench press me, who was covered in tattoos, and had dark hair sprinkled over his entire body. My perfect man also had a thick full beard that I could see speckles of gray in when I examined it closely. Only Sam would do for me.

As I sat on his lap, his eyes became dilated and his breathing sped up. I could feel his cock becoming hard, and mine reacted in turn. Sam and only Sam could coerce this sort of reaction out of me. With everyone else, I could get hard quickly, but only if I imagined Sam while I stroked myself or while someone gave me an awesome blow job. With Sam though, he simply had to touch me and my cock responded. And over the past month, my favorite visual and memory was him lying in bed, naked with one arm behind his head and his tattoos on display for me. No sheet or blanket hiding his body from my eyes. I could see everything. The way his dick rested between his legs—one leg was bent to give me a better view—and the peaks and valleys of his hard body.

My breathing became erratic and we hadn't done anything yet. That was about to change.

Smashing my mouth against his, I kissed him. It wasn't sweet or polite. It was rough and tumble, more like a WWE cage match than two

164

lovers kissing. After everything we'd been through, we could do sweet and romantic later. I needed him here, now, hard, fast, messy, and utterly satisfying.

Sam growled into my mouth at the same time one of his hands grabbed my hair and pulled. Our lips disengaged and my neck was exposed. Closing my eyes, my body trembled when he licked and sucked the side of my neck, close to my Adam's apple. He would leave a mark, everyone would know I belonged to him, and I became desperate for him to mark me everywhere.

His beard tickled my skin as Sam opened and closed his jaw, and then again when he moved from that spot, his lips and tongue leaving a wet trail as he moved down to my shoulder. Sucking and biting, leaving his mark there as well.

I whimpered. Every time he sucked, my hips instinctively thrust forward to grind our dicks together. I couldn't get close enough. I desperately craved more. Demanded more.

My hands gripped his t-shirt and fisted it, pulling and twisting the material. Fuck. I still felt a little lightheaded, but I didn't know if it was the hangover or my desire for him talking. My body was greedy and cried with need.

Letting go of his shirt, I began lifting it over his head. He disengaged his mouth so that I could pull it over his head. And then I removed mine, but it still wasn't enough. If anything, I was greedier. We had been separated a matter of weeks, and it may as well have been a lifetime.

"Fuck," he gasped. "Lube?"

"Huh?" I couldn't think, and therefore, he could not expect me to answer any question right now. He could probably ask if I was pregnant and I'd say yes if it got his dick in my ass.

"Babe, work with me here. Where's the lube?"

I frowned and stared into his eyes for a moment before the last word finally registered. "Bedroom." With his impending trip, I'd run to the store and made sure I had plenty—15 tubes. We'd go through it eventually. I thought about hiding some here in the living room, but I wasn't sure where to put it without my roommate, the neat freak, finding it. I was surprised he allowed the dining room table to look as haphazard as it did.

There wasn't enough room to get my ankles behind his back, so I shuffled off of him and ran to my room. Opening my nightstand drawer to pull one of the tubes out, I found it empty. "Shit." It should've been there. Where the fuck was the multitude of lube I bought?

"What's wrong?" Sam's hands glided to my shoulders and began to knead them.

I leaned back against him, throwing my head back, and closing my eyes to revel in the feel of him behind me. Reaching back to pull him closer, I found bare skin. My hands stretched beyond his hips to his butt mound, no clothing obstructing my quest.

"What's wrong, Josh?"

Again, I didn't understand how he expected me to follow any fluid train of thought except my desperate need for him to fuck me. Damn, the lube. "It's not here."

"What's not?" He must be having the same issues, because there was only one reason to run to my bedroom when I'd rather have stayed on his lap.

"The lube. I could have sworn I put it in this drawer."

"Don't worry about it. I came prepared. I swear the TSA agent gave me the funniest look when he inspected my bag."

I almost fell backward when he left me momentarily to ruffle through his bag. It only took him a moment before he turned around and smirked. "Strip and get on the bed."

I wasted no more time and pulled everything off, tripping in my excitement and landing on the bed. Lifting my foot, I ripped the offending jeans off and scooted backward. I rested my head on one of the pillows, waiting for my fiancé to join me.

Fiancé. That word made my gut clench and gave me a thrill of excitement and lust. Mine. Forever. Three years ago, after I thrust the letter into his hand and ran away from everything in Imperial, I never thought for a moment that I would find myself engaged to the teacher I had fallen in love with. It wasn't supposed to happen, but it did.

"What are you thinking about?" Sam asked as he climbed onto the bed beside me.

Funny, five minutes ago I couldn't focus. I kept thinking about the new dynamics of our relationship, and now I couldn't get the thought out of my head. This man was mine, and he would stand beside me throughout our lives. I'd never experienced such happiness before. "Us."

He leaned down, his lips hovering over mine as he whispered, "It's a good thing to think about," and then he kissed me.

The desperation from minutes ago returned with a vengeance when his tongue flicked over mine. Grunting beneath him, I reached up and held his neck, digging my fingers into the skin and the light curl there. And when I felt his hand snaking past my balls, I spread my legs wide and lifted my hips a little to give him better access.

One finger breached the tight muscles, and I accidentally bit his lip, hissing in pleasure. There was a slight burn that quickly disappeared. "Sam, I don't want slow and steady."

He pulled his finger out and added another one, pumping them both in and out of my hole. When I began to bear down on his fingers, fucking myself, he scissored them, stretching me further.

It still wasn't enough for me. There was a slight pleasure/pain and a small burn, but I wanted him to bury himself to the hilt deep inside me, as far as he could go. "Sam," I whined, begging him to stop using his fingers and to start using his cock.

Flipping me over onto my stomach, he slapped my ass and I yelped. "Get on your hands and knees," he ordered.

Behind me, I felt the cool liquid of more lube dripping between my orbs, and then his fingers dove in again. But they didn't stay. They were quickly replaced with his dick rubbing against me before it pressed against me, pressuring my hole to submit. And it did. The crown of his cock slid in and he stopped.

It had been a while since we'd been together and this was the biggest thing I'd had in me since I left Missouri. But I didn't want him to stop. Pressing back against him, he pushed forward, and we met in the middle. I felt full again. God I'd missed this. I hummed in pleasure.

He withdrew slightly and then thrust in deeper, but his pace was too slow, too careful, and it pissed me off.

"Can you stop acting like I'm delicate and start actually fucking me?" I snapped.

His laugh vibrated next to my ear, sending a shiver down my spine. "Your wish is my command."

"Does that mean you'll start calling me ma—?" My question ended with a howl when he thrust forward with so much power, my arms gave out on me and I was pushed face first into the mattress. Heaven.

In answer, he chuckled, pulled back and sank back in as far as he could. He kept up that pace. Hard and fast. And I loved it.

I grabbed my dick when I could already feel the tingle building within me. Pumping myself in time with his thrusts, I rushed to the edge of orgasm. "Coming. Come with me," I stammered breathlessly.

"Together," he groaned, his thrusts getting harder and jerkier.

I couldn't hold off any longer and succumbed to my climax, making a mess of my hand and my blanket. And he followed me with one last thrust.

I doubted I would ever get enough of him. I wasn't sure how, but every time was better and better regardless if it was slow or frenzied. This was us, who we were together, and I wouldn't change a thing. This was the man I was going to spend the rest of my life loving; I couldn't wait to start forever with him.

"I love you," I mumbled, trying to catch my breath.

Pulling out of me, he kissed the back of my neck. "I love you too."

"Forever."

"Yeah, forever."

Chapter 16

Joshua

Bright and early Monday morning, we went down to the local courthouse, and true to Sam's research, we didn't have to wait for our marriage license. Even though I lived in Florida, because I was still technically a resident of Missouri, with a Missouri driver's license, and paid out of state tuition, I wasn't considered a Florida resident. Jacob and another one of my friends, Chase, came down with us and we were married on the spot.

Without any fanfare and without my mother, we legally belonged to each other now. Oddly enough, I thought it was weirder to say I was married to him than it had been to say I was engaged. Joshua Dayton wedded to his ex-biology teacher. He even put in for a change of name. Samuel Cayden would cease to exist and would become Samuel Dayton.

Our reception was lunch after our wedding at Marie Livingston's Steakhouse, a quiet slightly upscale restaurant with hardwood floors and mirrors everywhere. It was small and had limited seating, one of those places that had the nice linen tablecloths covering the tables and everyone spoke in hushed tones. The food was good, and so was the company, especially the man to my right. My husband.

It was almost like any other day, except it wasn't. Today, I forever linked myself to someone. It was both overwhelming and peaceful at the same time.

This morning when I told Sam that Jacob would come with us in case we needed witnesses, I thought I'd have to perform the Heimlich maneuver when he choked on his eggs. I got the distinct impression that he wasn't thrilled with the plan; however, there really weren't a lot of friends to choose from. Many had gone home for the summer, and if they weren't they were either working or going to school, and my roommate was supposed to be gone for another week visiting his own family. I had three friends who could come, which wound up only being two since Chris got food poisoning over the weekend.

I wouldn't say that Sam completely accepted Jacob's presence, but he also didn't run my friend off. I decided to count it as a win.

"So what now?" Jacob asked, his mouth full of steak, sitting directly across from me at our small square table tucked away in a dimly lit corner.

"What do you mean?" Sam questioned, his fork and knife hovering above his plate. Dropping them, he waited for Jacob to explain.

I had to admit, I didn't know exactly what he meant either, but I threw an answer out there anyway. "Sam's looking for a job and will be moving here. I guess we'll get a place together."

Rolling his eyes, Jacob shook his head. "That's not what I meant." At least this time he wasn't talking around a mouthful of food.

"Then what do you mean?" I closed my eyes for a moment and took a deep breath. I wasn't sure why, but his roundabout answers were frustrating me, which pissed me off because this was supposed to be an incredible day.

Sam dropped his hand to my knee and squeezed. As soon as we sat down, we both scooted our seats toward the corner so that we could sit as close as possible to each other. I covered his hand with my own, linking our fingers together, neither one of us taking our eyes from Jacob.

"Didn't you say something about daddy dearest forcing him to marry some woman? Isn't that why you two got married?"

While that might have been part of it—to protect Sam from anything his father had planned—it was not the only reason we got married. Jacob did have a point though.

Moving my gaze from Jacob, who was looking at us expectantly, to Sam, I asked, "What are we going to do about him?"

"You made me promise something." Sam grinned, winking at me, as his hand squeezed mine. He remembered.

"I did."

"What?" Chase asked between bites of food. The way he was shoveling it in, someone might question when he'd last eaten. He barely spared us a glance before he returned his focus to his food. It was probably a good thing he played rugby with a local team regularly. Sadly, he ate this way all of the time. He was taller than me by at least half a foot, and built like a brick wall.

I pressed my lips together and bit them to hold them in place. I wanted to laugh. Sam's face had an expression of horror and disgust pasted on it. It was like he'd never seen someone eat like that before, and

I couldn't blame him. The first time I went out with Chase, I'd lost my appetite. It was like Sam was watching a horror movie and a train wreck at the same time.

I grabbed his face and turned it away from Chase sitting across from him, but his eyes stayed glued, staring at my friend out of the corner of his eyes. "Focus, Babe."

Shaking his head, Sam concentrated, but couldn't help one last pained expression at Chase, shuddering as he did so. "I figured if you can get a couple of days off work and depending on when you have to go back out on the boat, we can take a short trip out there. I know you don't like to fly, but I'll be with you and I'll hold your hand the entire time. Although, it might be easier to simply call him and mail him a copy of our marriage certificate." His eyes wandered back to Chase, who was now trying to wave down our waitress in order to get more rolls and gravy, and Sam blanched, holding his hand over his mouth. He pushed his plate away, his steak only half eaten.

"Are you done?" Chase looked from the plate to my husband.

"Uh, yeah. You can have it." Sam stated, his voice strained.

Chase picked up Sam's plate and placed it to the side of him since he had yet to finish his own meal.

Shuddering again, Sam closed his eyes and did not open them again until they were focused on me. He held up his hand to shield himself from the spectacle across from him. "Why don't we just airmail it and not worry about him any longer." His words sounded forced, and his eyes kept darting toward his hand, but thankfully there was a blockade. Unfortunately, we didn't have ear plugs. Chase was not the person you took to a fancy restaurant. He was a good guy and a good friend, but his eating habits left a lot to be desired.

Jacob cackled. "You should see him during a pie eating contest. He holds the record, and he wins for our frat every year."

Without turning around, Sam nodded. "I'm so happy for you." The sarcasm dripped off his tongue, and he stuck his tongue out at me as he winked again. "I'm leaving the decision to you."

I bit my lip and stared into his hazel eyes. Up to me. For some reason, thinking about it felt daunting.

"Don't worry about answering right away. We'll figure it out." Sam's fingers brushed my cheek and cupped the back of my neck to pull me in for a short kiss.

"Okay." Part of me wanted to take our marriage certificate and shove it up Marcus's ass myself. To see his face when he realized his son was beyond his reach. And yet, part of me wanted to close the door and never think about Sam's family again.

Leaning in, I kissed him again. I loved the feel of his lips on mine...on me. But our bubble was popped by the sound of multiple people clearing their throats. Breaking apart, I could see our waitress standing next to Chase, staring at us with a smile on her lips. Jacob's hand covered his mouth and he appeared ready to laugh—asshole. And Chase sat there grinning at us.

"You may want to remember where you're at," Jacob told us, but then did something I hadn't been expecting. He started clapping, and Chase joined in.

My cheeks felt hot and I was sure they were tinged red, and Sam kissed me on my temple. But my embarrassment wasn't over yet. Jacob pushed his chair back, the legs scraping against the wooden floor. Holding up his beer, he announced to the restaurant, "I've never seen you happier, Josh. Sam, you take care of him. Congrats to the groom and...uh, groom."

Others in the restaurant joined in with his toast, lifting their glasses and echoing their felicitations. And my face burned brighter than it ever had in my entire life. I buried it in Sam's shoulder and could feel his body shake and hear his laugh, but the pink tinge of his neck gave away his embarrassment.

Our waitress brought us a bottle of champagne to congratulate us, and we gladly accepted, because it would have been rude at that point not to accept. Honestly, though, I had tonight off and I wanted nothing more than to go back to my empty apartment and spend some quality time alone with a very naked Sam. He wasn't going to be picking up the keys for his friend's house until next week when we got back from Missouri, so for now, we would use my place to do whatever we wanted, wherever we wanted. What my roommate didn't know, wouldn't hurt him.

After the toasts, and after we dropped off our witnesses, Sam took me home. And as we closed the door to my apartment, I said, "Let's overnight it to him and make the signature a requirement. That way we know he got it. We can send it on our way to the airport. I can't believe I'm getting on a plane."

"For me."

"It's about the only reason I would."

His smile was blinding and it made my breath catch. His teeth were practically glowing white against the dark brown of his beard. And his laugh lines deepened around his eyes. "Are you sure about only overnighting it?"

"Yeah." I smiled. "We'll send it and then forget about him." As much as I wanted to see Marcus Cayden turn colors like a mood ring, to see his reaction when he realized he could no longer touch Sam, it wasn't worth it. Suffering on a plane to go to both California and Missouri, taking more time off work, it just wasn't worth any of the stress it would cause.

He slapped his hands against my cheeks and jerked me toward him, pressing his lips to mine in a mind blowing kiss. Spinning me around, he slammed me against the wall near the kitchen, our lips never separating.

When he finally released my mouth, we were both breathing hard and he pressed his forehead against mine. "I love you."

"Love you too," I whispered breathlessly. I couldn't do anything more than that.

Sam smiled and kissed me again. Not as hard or long, but still toe curling. And this time when we separated, he pushed me towards the bedroom to begin our wedding night celebration in the middle of the day.

Hard to believe that almost six years ago, I fell in love with my teacher. Three years ago, I confessed. And a couple of short months ago, he became mine. We weren't perfect, but we loved each other. Some probably considered our relationship out of the ordinary, or thought that we had moved too quickly, but who wanted ordinary? It was like my father once said, "When you know, sometimes, you know."

This was us, and I wouldn't change a thing. Our journey made us into who we were, and brought us to this moment together. Three years ago, he wouldn't have been ready. Hell, I didn't know if I would've been.

We probably had more obstacles ahead, and we still had a lot to learn about each other, but we were together. Right now. This was our time, and we planned on taking full advantage of it.

THE END

Acknowledgements

Life is about change, and sometimes we need to remember that not everything is as it appears.

The past year has taken me on an incredible journey and I've met so many wonderful people because of it. I've grown as an author and as a person. It makes me excited about the future.

This book was definitely a learning experience, and I want to thank everyone who helped make my first MM possible.

To my family, thank you for always having my back, for your support and encouragement, and for being there when my life completely changed. I wouldn't have made it without you. You're support in my writing journey is precious and cherished.

To Shana Vanterpool, thank you for being a friend and wonderful editor. You are truly an inspiration and mentor. I love your books, your spirit, and your friendship. Not to mention your good taste in abs. You are amazing. You helped me get my story out there and believed in me when I told you I wanted to write an MM. Thank you. Spencer says hi to Bella. (Everyone reading this, if you have not read her work, DO IT!!)

To Z.B. Heller, you are truly amazing! You helped encourage me and guided me through this entire process. I couldn't ask for a better mentor as I take this step into MM. Thank you for everything! #friendshipgoals

To Tiffany Black and T.E. Black Designs, the cover for By the Book turned into something breathtaking. You surpassed the vision I had for it and made it so much more. I am forever grateful to you and your creations.

To Christopher John at CJC Photography. Your work is amazing and I'm ecstatic that I got to work with you on this project. Plus, you encouraged me when I was getting frustrated with it. Thank you!

To TankJoey and Connor Jay, the perfect models and muses for this book. Thank you for gracing my cover.

To the girls at Smokin' Hot Reads Book Blog: Jamie, Krista, and Melissa. You are the best. You showed me the ropes, encouraged me, and are some of the greatest friends I could ever ask for. Krista, I want more dirty ditties (we need to get you published). Love you. Jamie, your friendship and support mean more to me than you will ever know. Thank you for inviting me to join the blog. Melissa, thank you for helping me with the learning curve and always encouraging me.

To Becky, Melissa, Tania, and Sharon. Thank you for beta reading for me. I couldn't have done this without you.

To Becky, you have continued to support me, kick my butt when I needed it, and you are the best proofreader a girl could have. Don't worry, the Viking story is coming. I promise it is.

To Courtney (aka other Maria. LOL.), thank you for everything! You helped make this story even better. I am forever grateful to you for all of your help.

To Jackie, THANK YOU!! I know you don't think you do much for me, but you are the best PA in the world. It's the little things that keep me sane. I'm so glad we found each other and became friends. You are a godsend.

To the countless blogs and people that have helped to promote By the Book, thank you!! Without you, indie authors would get little exposure. You help keep our community growing and spreading. Thank you for getting the word out.

To my high school creative writing teacher, Mrs. Shelton, you always encouraged me to go for my dreams, and I will forever be grateful. Under your guidance, I learned so much about myself and my writing.

To my friends, you are the best. After I got sick, you were there for me, and picked me up when I felt discouraged. You helped me to remember that I was not alone, that you were right there with me.

To Joyce, we have been best friends since we were kids, and I hope we continue to be best friends throughout our life. You have always kept it real with me and told me when I was being an idiot, but with my writing, you did nothing except encourage me. You told me I could do it and when I got frustrated, you listened to me gripe. You have been there from the beginning, and were one of the people who told me I could publish a book back in high school. I love you.

To the Love Seekers, you're support means the world. I started my reader group as a place to post what I wanted when I wanted, and it was grown from there. I have found friendships and have fun in that group on a daily basis. Thank you for that, for everything.

To the people in the world who battle autoimmune diseases. We are many and it is a struggle, but you battle it out every day and are my heroes. Keep fighting, and when you can't fight, lean on your friends. We'll support you.

To my readers of my books and of my fanfiction, thank you for reading my work and for supporting me. You will forever hold a special place in my heart.

Everyone, thank you for believing in me.

About the Author

Maria Vickers currently lives in St. Louis, MO with her pug, Spencer Tracy. She has always had a passion for writing, and after she became disabled, she decided to use writing as her escape.

She has learned a lot about life and herself after becoming sick. One of the things she has learned and lives by is, life is about what you make of it. You have to live it to the fullest no matter the circumstances.

Connect with Maria

Facebook: https://www.facebook.com/mariavickersbooks/

Instagram: @authormariavickers

Twitter: @mvauthor

Amazon: http://tinyurl.com/mvickersamazon

Goodreads: http://tinyurl.com/mvickersgoodreads

Newsletter: http://eepurl.com/cvH8tX

Join Maria's Love Seekers:
https://www.facebook.com/groups/1362108480474447/

Other Books by Maria

Another Chance
http://a.co/g3p32b4

Exposed: Book One of the Love Seekers Series
(Can be read as a standalone)
http://a.co/evU1CpW

Redeemed: Book Two of the Love Seekers Series
(Can be read as a standalone)
http://a.co/2VnZkvi

Made in the USA
Middletown, DE
22 July 2017